THE BERLIN UPRISING

RICHARD WAKE

MANOR AND STATE, LLC

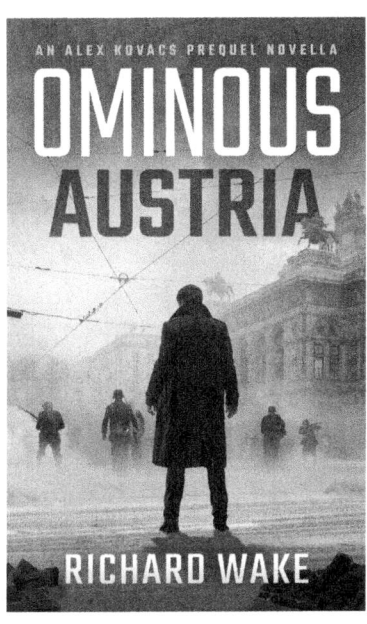

PART I

JUNE 2

1

Friedrichshain in 1953 was like most neighborhoods in East Berlin after the war, only more so. That is, bombed to hell by the Allies and barely rebuilt — at least, barely rebuilt in the parts where the people actually lived. On so many streets, eight years later, there were still the reminders of the destruction and especially its randomness. There would be two or three apartment buildings on the block, and maybe the right half of the first one and the left half of the third one would be obliterated, just piles of bricks and worthless whatnot — because all of the valuable whatnot would have been long-since scooped up by scavengers. Often the bricks were gone, too, leaving vacant lots, and people would be living in what was left, tarps covering some of the windows, buckets catching the roof leaks, barely getting by. A good metaphor for the city.

"Like sentinels standing watch for the future," is how a pair of those buildings on Singerstrasse were described in a picture caption in *Neues Deutschland*, the newspaper where I told the rest of them that I was working as a copy editor. Behind the busted-up houses in the photograph were construction cranes working on some project on Stalinallee and, well, I told them that I was the one who wrote the caption and I received a prized attaboy the next day — a tear sheet stuffed into my cubbyhole from the boss with a red grease pencil circle around the caption and the single word, "Good!" I couldn't believe how easily I embroidered the entire fake scene.

"You really are a kiss-ass," said my imaginary desk mate, Hans. The rest of them had already heard about Hans, about his imaginary dandruff and his imaginary habit of picking his nose while he edited copy and eating what he had excavated.

"You know, that wasn't my original caption," I said to Hans in an imaginary reply.

"What was the original?"

"'Summer teeth'."

"I don't get it."

"Imagine a smile," I said, holding up the picture with the buildings and the empty spaces between them. "Summer teeth. Some are there, some are there."

The three of them — Gerd the concrete mason, Hansi the pipefitter, and Freddy the glazier — roared their approval. Then Gerd grabbed my left wrist and said, "You might have hands as soft as a baby's behind but you are one funny asshole."

Sometimes I couldn't believe how easily I had inserted myself into their world. I was in a bar that night in one of the summer teeth on Lange Strasse. The place was called The Aerie, which had to have been a joke even before the war, seeing how it was darker and smokier than any bar I could remember. Karl was behind the bar as always, working beneath a sign that proclaimed him, "Owner, Bartender and Asskicker." It was the kind of bar where, as Karl himself said, "If I don't have to break up at least one fight a night, it's like it wasn't really a night at all."

Gerd, Hansi and Freddy were all shop stewards in their respective unions. One time, I asked Gerd how you got to be a shop steward and he said, "In my case, it was because I had a cold and skipped the meeting."

"Elected in absentia," I said.

"There's a life lesson in there somewhere," he said.

The truth was, Gerd was the sharpest of the three of them and the biggest firebrand. Hansi was kind of pathetic, torn, vacillating. Freddy was cautious but seemed as if he could be counted on. And I was playing my part: Alex Kovacs, an analytical crusading journalist who could be none of those things — not analytical, not crusading, not a journalist, not really — seeing as how I was a copy editor for one of the two East Berlin newspapers, both of which were controlled by the party.

But it was all fiction. I had never set foot in the offices of *Neues Deutschland*. What I knew about newspapers came from the stories my best friend Leon, a journalist in Vienna, told me. Most of them were old stories, though, and Leon was kind of a bullshitter sometimes, and I occasionally wondered exactly how far onto the thin ice I was venturing. Nobody at the table had caught on yet, though, and it had been more than a month.

I took a chance the first time. A small chance, but a chance. I mean, what if one of them had known somebody on the staff at the paper? I would have been sunk before I had started and headed back to Vienna with my dick in my hand, the mission ruined. But it had worked out, and they bought the rest of the backstory that I had worked out with Fritz, my handler with the Gehlen Org.

"You know what your problem's going to be?" he said.

"No, what?"

"Your goddamn Vienna accent."

"Which is really kind of a Strasbourg accent."

"I know. The maid taught you growing up in Brno or some shit. Rich kid."

"You done?" I said.

"I guess," Fritz said. "Anyway, here's your story. Your family was from Stuttgart, and your parents split up, and your mother was dead, and you were in the home guard near, I don't know, Dresden. You somehow got a letter from your 68-year-old father that he came to Berlin to defend his man Adolf. Never heard from him again. You figure he got killed in '45 in a bombing in a place like Friedrichshain — that's where he said he was living in the letter. After the war, well, there was nothing left for you in Stuttgart so you came here — you know, maybe to find him — and when you didn't find him, you just stayed. Voilà. Accent explained."

And that's the story I told them on the night I walked into The Aerie. I came, I looked for my father, I stayed. I wove a story about a father who actually didn't like me very much, who was always closer to my younger brother — which wasn't that much of a fiction when it came to my real backstory.

"Still, I felt like I had to look," I told them. "I know it's a little fucked up, but..."

"Not so fucked up," Gerd said.

"No?"

"One last chance to try to please him," he said. That was my first inkling that he was the sharpest of the three of them.

So we drank that night, the four of us, and swapped affectionate stories about what assholes our fathers were. The fathers were all dead now, mine included. The other three were all fathers now themselves and all insistent that they had learned from their own fathers' mistakes. I was the only single man in the group.

"There was a woman in Stuttgart," I said.

"You could go back — just hop on the U-Bahn and get off in West Berlin," Hansi said.

"I know, I know. It's just..."

I drank. They all nodded and drank, too.

Anyway, I told them I had worked at the paper in Stuttgart before the war, and I knocked on the door at *Neues Deutschland*, and, well, whatever. They bought it all. I knew by the second week, when they saw me and shouted my name and waved me over to their table, that I was in. Every Friday since then, I had become a regular. I heard about their jobs and their kids and their whispered disdain for the party. I commiserated with them and laughed with them and, as a group, we ducked more than one beer mug thrown in anger. They almost always came from the far left corner of the bar.

"Steamfitters," Freddy said, after Karl had restored order one night. "Always the damn steamfitters."

2

"The price of everything is up," Hansi said.

"And we're fucking starving as it is," Freddy said.

"And now this 10 percent bullshit on top," Gerd said.

"Bullshit is right — it can't continue," I said. "I doodled this at work today. Just in the last three months, here's what has happened to the price of pork, potatoes and anything green."

"There's nothing green anymore except spoiled pork and potatoes," Hansi said.

I showed them the paper, my little bit of ciphering.

"You guys say there's almost no more overtime at the building site, right?" I said.

They all nodded.

"Only thing that kept our heads above water," Freddy said.

They all nodded again.

"The food prices are up 20 percent, there's no more overtime, and now you have the 10 percent work quota on top. Ten percent more work for the same wage."

They all stared at my figuring.

"Can't fucking continue," Gerd said.

"I don't see how," I said.

That was my job, to stir the pot in as unobtrusive a manner as possible. I had been doing it since the second week in The Aerie. A word of encouragement here or there. A question designed to elicit discontent one week. Or, maybe, a made-up example of anti-worker sentiment within the party that I had heard second-hand in the newspaper office. Always, though, the same punctuation.

It can't fucking continue.

I don't see how.

These were the heads of three of the unions that worked on Stalinallee Block 40, one of the monstrous new building projects along the big, wide boulevard that was supposed to show the rest of the world what a grand and modern workers' paradise East Germany was becoming. Everybody knew, of course, that nobody who worked with their hands was ever going to live in one of the new apartments — and that two or three blocks behind the gigantic white wedding cakes along Stalinallee were the streets with the summer teeth where the real East Berliners lived. You know, the places where food was short, and running water and electricity were intermittent, and heat was a rumor.

This was the life these guys lived, Gerd and Hansi and Freddy. They lived it and their men lived it. Ever since the party announced the changes in the economic plan in March, well, the party was headed by Walter Ulbricht and Otto Grotewohl, and they became universally known as Fucking Ulbricht and Fucking Grotewohl, and not always in a whisper.

People's standard of living really did drop by about a third overnight — it was already a hard life before the changes, and now it was becoming intolerable. The 10 percent quota was clearly the most galling part, too. Extra work that had been performed for overtime was now being done for free.

"Voluntary, they said," Hansi said.

"Voluntary, my ass," Freddy said.

"And mandatory at the end of the month," Gerd said.

"Hard to see how it will stick," I said.

"Fucking right," they all mumbled, kind of.

When it was my turn to get the pitcher, I would always use the bathroom and then take my time at the bar. It would give me a chance to eavesdrop. Over the course of several weeks, there were exactly three kinds of conversations in that union workers' bar that I would catch snatches of. The men would talk about women they weren't sleeping with, or the football team that was letting them down, or the quotas. That really was it.

And if I heard it in those brief interludes on Friday nights, then Gerd, Hansi and Freddy likely heard it all day, every day. Part of me wondered if I really was going to have to do anything except be a cheerleader from the sideline that was The Aerie. Buy my pitchers, lend a sympathetic ear, offer a bit of encouragement, fin.

Maybe.

When the punches started flying and the pitchers began crashing — the steamfitters, again — I made my excuses and walked home to my flat. The street lights were like everything else in East Berlin, flickering on and off, but I managed not to face-plant. It wasn't that long of a walk, just 10 minutes or so. The streets were quiet. I always got the impression that the guys in the bar were mostly single and in their twenties, which meant that they had fewer responsibilities and a bit of ready cash. But for family men, well, there really wasn't a whole lot of disposable income anymore. Friday nights out with the wife had become monthly dates rather than weekly for most of them. Gerd admitted to me that the only reason he and Hansi and Freddy could afford their Friday nights at The Aerie was because of the small stipend they received as shop stewards.

When I got done climbing up to my flat on the top floor —

no lights evident in any of the other flats — I opened the door and saw the note from Rolf, the super. It was, as always, written on a piece of light blue paper that had been folded in half. Rolf's handwriting was small and precise. How he received the messages in the first place, I had no idea and I never asked — not that he would tell me. Need to know and all that. But however he got them, Rolf passed them along, and then I burned the paper in the sink.

The meeting was in Lichterfelde West at 11 a.m. the next day. West Berlin. Fritz?

PART II

JUNE 3

3

Fritz Ritter was second in command at the Gehlen Org, which meant he should have been sitting behind a desk at the compound outside of Munich, coordinating the intelligence gathered behind the Iron Curtain that was being sold to the Americans and sipping schnapps with Reinhard Gehlen himself. Except he never was. I had no idea how many agents Fritz ran besides me. For all I knew, I was the only one at the point. He was well into his seventies and starting to look it. He really did belong behind a desk at that point, not in the field.

Then again, as I entered the gate of the botanical garden and began my wandering back to toward the big greenhouse building where all the tropical plants were, I saw Fritz sitting instead in a chair near the entrance. He was beside some bushes, his head tilted back to catch the sun, and he didn't look out of place at all.

When he heard the gravel crunch beneath my feet, Fritz didn't open his eyes immediately and instead pointed to the empty chair next to him.

"What, not all the way in the back this time?" I said.

"A big place. Plenty to see. Were you followed?"

"Don't think so."

"No greater assurance than 'don't think so'?"

"Not my town. Best I can do."

"Do you have a town anymore?" Fritz said.

Vienna was still my town, but I took his point. Vienna, actually, was a place where I laid my head between assignments, and caught up with my best/only friend Leon, and waited for Fritz to take the train in from Munich to brief me on what was next. Other than that, I had no life in the town where I grew from high school to maturity.

After the war — the first war — my Uncle Otto had taught me how to be a traveling sales representative for the family mining company in Vienna, and I made a lot of money there both from the business and from what I inherited after Otto died. The fact that Fritz was Otto's friend, and that Otto had been collateral damage when a Gestapo officer began to sniff out that Fritz — an Abwehr general — was working against the Nazis, tied Fritz and I together in the nearly 20 years since. Sometimes it was comfortable, almost loving. Sometimes it was cynical — beyond cynical. I went years not knowing what to think about the relationship, but that was mostly earlier. For better or worse, I had made my peace with the whole thing in the years after the second war. I guess I just figured that even if I had no family left, well, I still had him.

Fritz had closed his eyes again, and then he opened them, and then he rubbed him, and then he pointed at the bush that was about 10 feet in front of where we sat.

"I love this, the color of the berries," he said.

"You mean orange?"

"Look closer. It's kind of orange but it's kind of red, too. A very unique color. Look closely."

"Orange, red, got it."

"Common sea buckthorn," Fritz said. "You can brew a tea out of the berries. Tastes okay. And if you're a little stopped up, colon-wise, it really keeps things moving, if you know what I mean."

"How do you know so much about this shit?"

"Always have. We had a great garden at our house."

"Where was that again?" I said.

"Bamberg. Well, just outside. A nice house, tidy, with a big garden. Winnie loved it. Real green thumb."

"Who knew?"

"What exactly do you know about me?" Fritz said.

He closed his eyes again, and the question kind of hung there. I was treating it as rhetorical because I wasn't in the mood for much more. What did I know about him? I knew what he told me, basically. I knew that he and my uncle met in the 1920s while occupying adjacent barstools, an itinerant sales rep and a traveling inspector of military installations united in their pursuit of women on the road. I also knew that Fritz used me once to save his own ass from the Gestapo, and that he saved mine a half-dozen times in return, and that he now sent me out on dangerous missions for the greater good of gathering intelligence to hurt the Commies in whatever country they existed. Oh, and also building up the Gehlen Org so that it would be in position to take over as West Germany's intelligence arm whenever the Allies got around to allowing them to have their own spies.

"You must have at least one more ass-chasing story with Otto that you haven't told me," I said.

Eyes closed, Fritz waved his hand — and the request — away. He usually liked to tell those stories. Maybe it was because he'd just brought up his wife and the big garden in Bamberg.

"We do have some business," he said. Eyes open now, sitting up straight.

My eyes were closed now.

"Pay attention."

"Yup, yup." I was awake now, sitting up just as straight as he was.

At which point, Fritz added more to my plate. He started telling me about this Stasi major named Johannes Mundt. He was one of them but he was working for us, and what he was providing was information — color, mostly — on the East German party, and the big suits who ran it, and their dealings with the Soviets. "Personal stuff more than political stuff, but still useful," is how Fritz put it.

The guy from the Gehlen Org who had been running Mundt was somebody whom I had never met. That wasn't surprising. It wasn't like we all hung out in the lunchroom at Spies Inc. and traded office gossip, after all. Anyway, the guy had to go home and deal with an ailing wife, and so they needed me to step in.

"I mean, I am kind of busy already," I said.

"I've seen the reports. You're not exactly fucking breaking your back."

"I think I'm getting results."

"I do, too," Fritz said. "But you're in the bar with those guys like, maybe twice a week. The rest of the time, you've got your thumb up your ass. You have time to meet with this guy for me every now and again. First meeting is tomorrow."

I had been sent to Berlin for a purpose: to help foment resistance to the East German regime by stoking resentment among leaders of some of the building trades unions. As Fritz had said when he laid it out back when we were in Vienna, "Our overlords..."

"...you mean the Americans..." I said.

"...who, as you well know, pay the bills," Fritz said. "Our overlords want us to attempt to adjust the tension on the rubber band in East Berlin. They want us to try and see if we can make it snap."

And that's what I was doing, slowly at first, painstakingly, one beer at a time, one this-can't-continue at a time. I felt good about the momentum that was building, too, and now I knew that Fritz did, too.

"I just don't want to mess up the real mission," I said.

"You won't. Mundt is secondary. But you're here, and you do have the time, and I could use the help. And there's another thing."

"Do your laundry, too?"

"Just listen," Fritz said. "And this is important. Your two jobs are separate — completely, totally separate. You don't provide Mundt with any information about your other gig. You don't even tell him you have another gig. Don't trust him. Don't confide in him. Like, not even a little."

"You don't trust him?"

"About as far as I can throw him."

"Then why am I doing this?"

"Because the information has been solid so far," Fritz said. "Rock solid. And useful. Not like nuclear secrets or anything, but useful. Colorful. Helps paint a fuller picture. And like I said, rock solid so far. So, I put my mistrust to the side."

With that, he struggled to his feet and began walking toward the entrance of the botanical garden. The grunt as he got out of the chair was just a little bit louder this time than I remembered. His gait was just a little bit slower — not labored, not crazy slow, but slower. Just a little. A man aging.

Near the gate, we passed a forsythia. The branches were a little wild, untrimmed, and they still held a last bit of yellow.

"The spring was so cold, and they came out so late," Fritz said. "So unusual to see any yellow this late. Really, unheard of."

"I mean, they just grow like weeds, right?" I said.

"Kind of, but not exactly."

We walked a few more steps and then turned back.

"It's such a pretty yellow," Fritz said.

4

The train back from the botanical garden was actually two trains. I had to change at Friedrichstrasse, the massive station where so many of the spaghetti strands of the U-Bahn and the S-Bahn tangled together. The station was in the Soviet sector and, because so many trains from there headed into the British, American and French sectors, it was the place where the majority of those fleeing from East to West had to change trains. And so the place was crawling with not only regular flatfoots, the Vopo, but also Stasi men. All of them were looking for the telltale signs — that is, families carrying luggage bigger than a knapsack. If you were naive enough to play it that way, you were stopped, and you had your name taken, and you were sent back on a train heading back East. Everyone else, though, skated through. What could the cops do, after all?

It was against the rules but thousands of East Berliners commuted to unauthorized jobs in West Berlin every day, East Berliners who returned with West marks that were a lot more valuable than East marks. The country tried to shame them, but there was little the party could do given that the West currency was worth so much more on the black market. Money talked, then as always.

So, into an already crowded station came those fleeing East Germany for good. This was the doorway into the West, the only one in the country. Every other border crossing in the country was staffed and impossible to cross. Only there, in the mass confusion that was a typical day in Friedrichstrasse Station, was free passage from East to West — as long as you weren't traveling with a mattress strapped to your back. And the thing was, even if they did stop you and the mattress, you could just go back and try again the next day.

Anyway, nobody looked twice at me as I changed trains and headed toward the Ostbahnhof, the station nearest to my flat. One, because I was empty-handed. And, two, because I was headed East not West. The cops were all looking at the people walking down the steps from the platform, not the people walking up.

I honestly never even thought twice about taking the trains. What I did think about — and think about a lot — was the apartment. As Fritz had warned me ahead of time, "It's always the biggest issue in East Berlin — especially in East Berlin. It's getting worse in other places in the East, but they started the system in East Berlin and they perfected it. Those goddamned books."

If you needed to find a place for an agent in West Berlin, you just rented a vacant flat and called it a day. In the East, though — besides the fact that there were no vacant flats — was the problem of "The Book." In short, each apartment building had a superintendent of sorts — and besides the normal superintendent duties of fixing leaks and collecting the mail, there was another tax that was really Job 1 as far as the Stasi was concerned. That is, keeping "The Book."

What was in it? For each tenant — each father, mother and child — there was the normal name, birth date, and details from identity documents. But it was more than that. If a tenant had a visitor who spent more than three nights, the visitor's name was supposed to go into the book. That one wasn't hard and fast, you know, given the habits of single men and women — but in general nobody spent more than three nights without getting their name in the ledger.

So you couldn't, say, just give somebody a new roommate and not have it recorded. And if an apartment became vacant, you couldn't just slip somebody else into it because the book would show the change of identity and, well, housing was in such short supply that vacancies were like gold, and local party officials and councils doled them out in exchange for, if not gold then favors of some sort down the line.

Given all of that, it was one the Gehlen Org's great triumphs when they recruited Rolf Berner, therefore. Rolf was the super in my building.

"They're fresh, still a little warm — I grabbed a couple of extras from the stall in the station," I said, handing Rolf a couple of the rolls I had bought in the Ostbahnhof. It was the terminus for all of the trains that went east, and so it was always at least a little bit busy. Fritz always said, "You want busy. The last thing you want is a station out in the ass-end of nowhere, when a single, bored, nosy Vopo can really fuck things up."

Rolf was slow to answer the door when I knocked. He was getting slower all the time. Cancer. I didn't know what kind. He was kind of a private sort, and I was a little surprised he had told me as much as he did.

He pressed the bag of rolls against his cheek.

"Still warm," he said.

He thanked me but didn't ask me in, which was fine. The rolls were a courtesy, not a sign of friendship, if that made any sense. I didn't want to get any closer, mostly because every time I sat on his overstuffed couch and looked at his complexion growing paler and paler, the more I worried about having to find a new place to live. As he himself had warned me, "When the guy who keeps the book dies, all bets are off. It's not like what I did with poor Harald."

Poor Harald lived in my apartment before I did. Poor Harald liked the fellas, if you know what I mean. Poor Harald had been abandoned by his family because he liked the fellas. And one day, not that long ago, Poor Harald died of strangulation, and a young guy — likely one of the young guys who worked in the shadows on the street behind the Ostbahnhof, was heard to bound down the stairs in the middle of the night before Poor Harald's body was found.

Rolf liked Poor Harald but, well, what do they say? One man's tragedy is another man's opportunity. Rolf checked the book, just to make sure, but he already knew that Poor Harald had listed no next of kin. And so, in the middle of the next night, Rolf dragged Poor Harald's body down to the basement, and dug a hole in the earthen floor, and sentenced Poor Harald to an eternity spent beneath a stack of half-empty paint cans and a tangle of plumbing bits-and-bobs that might be recycled in a future repair project.

And, voilà. Alex Kovacs took the vacant apartment. If the Stasi or the Vopo ever checked, he was the new Poor Harald — and with the identity papers to prove it. And as for the other five people in the building? They were all old and tired, and you pretty much never saw them. In other words, not a problem and not likely to be a problem.

"Your best work," I said, when Rolf told me the story.

"That was nothing," Rolf said. "You should have met me before the diagnosis."

I heard everything but the last two words, but I could read

Rolf's lips. He strained to talk, but that wasn't the problem. It was the trains. We were so close to the station that you heard them all night. He had promised I wouldn't notice them after a week or two, but I did. Every goddamned night. Every goddamned train.

PART III

JUNE 4

5

I t was 285 steps to the viewing platform near the top of the Victory Column — I counted. I stopped once on the way up to catch my breath, and I was fully in need of another stop as I reached the top. Bent over, my chest heaving, a man in a blue business suit walked over, looked down at me, and said, "Christ... pathetic."

Thus did I meet Major Asshole, er, Johannes Mundt.

He walked away and found a spot along the railing, looking down on some palace. The viewing platform wasn't crowded but it wasn't empty, either. That is, about perfect for a meeting between spies. We wouldn't have to whisper and, at the same time, we wouldn't stand out.

"And why exactly are we doing this over here?" I said, attempting to regain a shred of my dignity by going on the conversational offensive. "I mean, honestly."

"Think about it," Mundt said.

"I have been. It's fucking stupid."

"It's not fucking stupid. It makes perfect sense. There are approximately a million places in East Berlin where I might run into somebody I know. West Berlin, not so much."

"But what if they saw you coming over? A bit suspicious, no?"

"They didn't see me coming over. And on the zillion-to-one chance that someone did, well, I'm just a sightseer on a beautiful day. Or I'm buying some French perfume for my wife's birthday, something you can't get on the other side. Or, whatever. But it's a zillion to one."

He paused, took a breath.

"Idiot," he said. "And why exactly do I have to fucking deal with you."

I told him the truth about his former contact and the sick wife. He sniffed.

"Some attention to duty," he said. "You people are so fucking soft."

In the span of about five minutes, Mundt had proven himself to be as big of an asshole as I had imagined. Bigger, actually. Fritz was going to owe me big for this, because it was obvious that every meeting with this prick was going to be an ordeal.

"So, what's this about?" I said, trying to move things along. "What's the word?"

"The word is that Ulbricht and Grotewohl were just in Moscow, and they went for the purpose of getting their asses chewed out."

I nodded. Ulbricht and Grotewohl were party bigwigs, the men in charge. I knew that much.

"It seems that the Soviets want Ulbricht to pretty much reverse course on everything he's been doing," Mundt said. "Like, everything — the whole fucking economic plan."

"Meaning?"

"Meaning less heavy industry and more clock radios and hair dryers instead," Mundt said. "Forget the collectivization of the farms. Forget stomping on the Protestant churches' necks. Consumer goods. Clock fucking radios. Forget the rest. And it wasn't a request, I don't think. The original plan was Stalin's but now he's dead. You have heard that Stalin's dead, right? You do know that much."

"Fuck you," I said with my eyes.

"Well, Khrushchev says to reverse course."

Mundt paused for emphasis.

"Or else," he said.

I didn't know shit, but this did seem like a big deal. I repeated the main points over in my head, quickly.

"What's the hurry?" I said.

Mundt replied with an exasperated sigh. Perfect asshole technique.

"Haven't they briefed you about anything?"

"Humor me." I wanted to say, "Humor me, asshole," but I didn't want to go there. Not yet, anyway.

"You know people are leaving East Germany, right?"

"On the U-Bahn," I said. "Yeah, yeah. So?"

"In the last day, do you want to know how many good citizens of the German Democratic Republic have fled to the West?" Mundt said. "About 1,000. That's been the average so far this year, 1,000 a day. Last year, it was 500 a day and that was considered a catastrophe. We are now into a double catastrophe. And most of them are highly educated — teachers, professionals, people like that."

"A thousand," I said, more to myself than to Mundt. Then I whistled softly.

"Exactly," he said. "It's a disaster for the country, and it's accelerating, and Moscow is worried. They're fucking worried as hell. And they all did it like we did today — get on the U-Bahn in the East and ride a few stops and get off in the West. As long as you're willing to leave empty-handed, there's nothing that can be done about it."

The major shrugged.

"You can seal the rest of the borders all you want, but this is the hole that everyone rushes through," he said. "We might turn back a handful a day, the ones who really look guilty, but that's it. And the truth is, they can just try again the next day."

"And the answer is clock radios and hair dryers?" I said.

"They don't know what the answer is," Mundt said. "But I guess they figure they have to try something."

We both looked out into the distance. Gardeners were cutting the grass at the palace below us, pushing mowers, three of them. Two other guys in the same green coveralls maneuvered big hedge clippers, shaping a line of bushes.

"So what's happening now?" I said.

"Meaning what?"

"Meaning, what's happening now that Ulbricht and Grotewohl have been given their new marching orders?"

"The Politburo is talking about it," Mundt said. "But they won't talk long. Semyonov won't let them."

"Who's Semyonov?"

"The fucking idiot they send me," he said. "Who's Semyonov? Vladimir Semyonov. Soviet High Commissioner. He's the Russian who's really in charge of everything."

"So Ulbricht doesn't really have the power?"

"He has as much power as Semyonov lets him have," Mundt said. And then, a throwaway out of the side of his mouth: "Fucking idiot."

I was too busy memorizing what Mundt was saying to be properly insulted by how Mundt was saying it. I kept getting stuck on Semyonov, but I figured Fritz would know who I was talking about if I came close with the pronunciation. Anyway, the properly insulted part would have to come later.

"Need me to repeat anything?"

"Fuck you."

"Witty comeback," Mundt said. He went on to provide me

the rest of his ground rules. He said that only he could contact me, and not the other way around. He said our next meeting would be at a café in Sachsenhausen at 2 p.m. the day after he left me the signal. The signal would be a chalk mark on the base of the lamp post on Hirtenstrasse that is just to the south of the Babylon Theater in Mitte.

"You know it?" he said.

"I'll find it," I said.

"Check every day after noon. It'll probably be in the next few days."

"Ass-end of nowhere, no? Sachsenhausen?" I said. I was suddenly thinking about Fritz and his one-bored-Vopo theory. I was also thinking about having to hoof it over to that theater every afternoon to check the lamp post.

"Not that far," Mundt said. "And not the camp itself. The café is on the road from the train station. A 10-minute walk, maybe."

6

I decided to visit The Aerie on a non-Friday night, just to see what it might be like and maybe to find out if there had been a hint of anything that Mundt had told me. When I walked in the door, the place was half empty but Karl was behind the bar, as always.

"You lose your calendar or something — it's only Thursday," he said.

"A man is thirsty when a man is thirsty."

"None of your friends are here."

"Then I'll drink alone," I said, grabbing the pitcher that Karl had begun pouring as soon as he saw me come through the door. I walked over to a table and parked myself. My back was to the back wall and my view included the entrance. Force of habit.

I had already left my own chalk mark for Fritz. Goddamned chalk marks. I had been using them since I learned the business of being a spy back in the 1930s and I was still using them in the 1950s. In that time, I had seen the radio transmitters shrink from suitcase-sized to pocket-sized. The invisible ink had morphed from lemon juice or some such thing to significantly more sophisticated chemical formulations. But the chalk remained the same, purchased from the school supply aisle of any department store in any city anywhere.

It remained effective because it was so innocent and so low-risk. What's the worst thing that could happen if a Vopo saw you marking a chalk X on a wall? He'd make you wipe it off while you told him a story about a girl you met in the same spot the night before. And if you somehow got arrested and got searched? A piece of chalk was a lot easier to explain away than a tiny transistor radio. For setting a meeting, there was no simpler, safer way.

I had done it first in Zurich in 1938. Jesus. There was this fountain with these mosaic tiles, and that's where I left and received requests for meetings with my contact. Make a mark, go to the meeting place at the pre-arranged time. See a mark, do the same. I did it in Zurich, did it in Prague, did it in more places than not. I don't know how many times I reached into my pants pocket for my keys and emerged with white fingers. It's why I always carried a handkerchief — to wipe my fingers as well as the inevitable white smudges on my suits.

Just as I had gone over the procedure with Major Asshole, I had also talked through it with Fritz the previous day. But I had a question.

"When I leave one for you, who checks the chalk mark? Not you, certainly."

"I have people for that," Fritz said.

"But if you have people, why do you need me to deal with the fucking major?"

"Because there are people whose level of competence tops out at the recognition of a chalk mark on the wall by the entrance to Track 2 in the Ostbahnhof, and then there are other people with a few more skills."

"Like me."

"Only a few more skills," Fritz said.

I would see him the next day. That night, I was just drinking, pretty much — drinking and maybe happening into a conversation with someone who might have gotten a sense of what Mundt had told me. Seeing as how I didn't know anybody in the bar except Karl, though, it was pretty much drinking. That is, until an attractive thirty-ish brunette approached my table.

"Hiding back here?" she said.

"I enjoy my privacy."

"Privacy in a public place?"

"The best kind of privacy — being around people without having to deal with people."

"A misanthrope, then?"

"Just a drinker," I said.

She sat down, she and her empty mug, and helped herself to my pitcher. As it turned out, her name was Elena and she was Gerd's sister. Karl had pointed me out at the bar.

"You come to this place alone?" I said.

"Sure, why not?"

I theatrically scanned the room and said, "Best as I can see, there is only one other woman in the place."

"Your point being?"

"Drunk men, few women, I don't know."

"What it means is that I have never paid for a drink in this place, never once. And," she said, clinking her mug against the pitcher, "my streak remains intact."

She smiled, I laughed. I liked her immediately. That I was old enough to be her, well, very much older brother, seemed not to matter. Of course, I was a few beers deep at that point, and the line between mattering and not mattering was blurring in the way that only alcohol can accomplish.

As I was then past the age of fifty, I was realistic about what I looked like. I wasn't fat, which was the most important thing when it came to attraction with the opposite sex. Older and fatter was fatal in these situations. Older and thin, though, could still work. The problem, which I had not anticipated, was that there was a downside to older-and-thinner that grew more pronounced every year. That is, a fat face looked younger than a thin face. The rest of you looked sloppy, but a fatter face hid time better. Given what I did for a living — the stress, the danger, the stretches without proper sleep and nutrition — all of that tended to show on my lean face, and around my eyes in particular. The rest of me looked pretty good, I had to admit — all except my eyes. The crow's feet were pronounced. The lines that radiated from my eyes, and also a bit along my cheeks, were deep. So I looked like I was in my fifties, but it was a handsome fifties. At least, that's what I told myself.

We chatted about our jobs mostly — hers as a bookkeeper for a trash hauling company, mine as the fictional copy editor at *Neues Deutschland*. She trotted out what must have been her go-to stories, including one about the trash truck driver who got caught disposing of the wife he had murdered, one limb at a time. He was caught when the truck went over a pothole and the head bounced out of the back and into the gutter.

"The kids in the neighborhood thought they had come upon a new football wrapped in brown paper," she said. "You know, until."

She had a couple of stories, and I repeated the stuff I had already told her brother and the rest, about my mythical desk mate and whatnot. The first pitcher turned into a second, and it was about half empty when Elena suddenly got to her feet.

"So soon?"

"Early work tomorrow. Inventory."

"Inventory of trash?"

"Trucks, truck parts, uniforms, stuff like that."

"Sounds fascinating."

"Pays the bills," she said. Pause. Then, "Do you like swimming?"

"Who doesn't?" I said. The truth was, I could swim barely well enough to save myself. Barely. My friend Leon once told me, "You swim like a panicky drunk — which, come to think of it..." There were likely five-year-olds who could beat me in a race. I probably hadn't been in a pool or a lake in 10 years.

Elena went on to talk about how much she liked to swim at Müggelsee, the big lake in East Berlin. "The water, the crowds, the families, the inclusiveness — I don't know," she said.

I didn't know, either, not first-hand, anyway. But *Neues Deutschland* was full of photographs from Müggelsee. A hot spell in May had prompted a full page of Müggelsee photos one day, people horsing around on paddle boats and kids eating ice cream and whatnot. Anyway, the weather on Saturday was supposed to be warm, and Elena wanted to know if I would meet her there.

"Say, 1 p.m.?" she said.

Yes, I said, without thinking. I assumed I would be able to buy a bathing suit in the next day.

PART IV

JUNE 5

7

I took the train the next day to Lichterfelde West, changing from one line to another at Friedrichstrasse, as always. As I descended the stairs from the one platform and headed across the station to the next — from the train leaving the East to the train entering the West — it might have been my imagination but it did seem as if there were a few more Vopo and/or Stasi people eying us up. I never worried then and never appeared to attract any attention. I was carrying nothing. My hands were in my pockets. I was whistling a kids' song I had heard that morning. The words were unbearable shit — "From the ruins risen newly, to the future turned, we stand. Let us serve your good weal truly, Germany, our fatherland" — but for some reason, I couldn't shake the tune. Anyway, nobody in a uniform seemed to notice me.

I had done some back-of-the-envelope math after talking to Mundt. If 1,000 people really were leaving a day — and they were mostly the better-educated citizens of East Germany — that would add up to, well, a ton. No country could survive such a brain drain. I didn't need the back of the envelope to understand that much.

When I got off the train at Lichterfelde West, I purposely walked for five minutes in the wrong direction, just because. When I arrived at the botanical garden, Fritz was again sitting on a bench near the entrance. Another bench, though, in front of another bush. This one was blue, or blue-green, not orange.

"You come a different way?" Fritz said.

"Every time."

"Anybody look at you funny?"

"The whole damn country looks at you funny when it isn't staring at its shoes," I said.

"Perhaps."

Fritz was on his feet and moving quickly. He was much more spry than the previous time we had met. Maybe old age came and went. I had begun to clock these things — like the observation about thin faces showing more of your age — and this was another thing I would mentally track. Anyway, we were walking along the path that would take us to this arboretum building deeper into the garden. The truth was, I didn't know what it was called. But it was a massive greenhouse kind of thing where hundreds of people could walk in the humidity.

First left, first right. Fritz was speeding up.

"A long fucking walk," I said.

"Not that long."

"Long enough."

"You're old before your time, you are," Fritz said.

Parents were pushing prams. Little kids riding little bikes or little scooters on the cinder paths. Old duffers were shuffling along. Two wedding couples were being dragged around by insistent photographers. When we got to the big glass structure and walked inside, the humidity hit you. A damp film coated everything — the plant leaves, the little granite benches, and the stepping stones over which you crossed the ponds to reach the next collection of horticultural whatever.

For some reason, walking across the stones scared me. Fritz positively skipped along while each step I took was profoundly fearful.

"Christ, just walk," Fritz said.

"I'm coming, old man."

"You'd come faster if you weren't always hung-over."

"Got me there," I thought to myself.

Eventually, Fritz stopped and pointed out a little tree at the end, and offered a quick dissertation on its properties. I didn't get the name: *Latinnus bullshittus*, whatever. When we finally sat down, Fritz pointed out some fern-like things across from the bench. I didn't hear anything he said, mostly because I was preoccupied by how wet my ass felt from the dew on the stone bench.

"So?" Fritz said.

At which point, I told him everything that Mundt had told me — about Ulbricht and Grotewohl getting called to Moscow to get their asses handed to them, and about the clock radios and hair dryers, and about the 1,000 a day who were leaving through Friedrichstrasse. Fritz stopped me there.

"That's their estimate, 1,000 a day?"

I nodded.

Fritz whistled softly.

"Oh yeah," I said. And even though I butchered Semyonov's name, I was able to get across to him that the Soviets' grand high executioner, or whatever his title was, wasn't going to allow Ulbricht and Grotewohl to screw around for very long before they would have to implement the orders.

Fritz took it all in. He whistled softly again.

"Well, that's some shit," he said.

"Important shit?"

"What do you think?"

"I'm not paid to think."

"Thankfully," Fritz said. He smiled widely.

"What do you think of the major?" he said.

"You mean, the major asshole?"

"Yeah. But besides that."

"What's there to think?" I said. "A dick is a dick."

"But the information?"

"You're the judge of that. I'm just the messenger."

Fritz paused again. The truth was, I really didn't know how important a change in industrial policy in East Germany either was or wasn't. I didn't know how important the status of Ulbricht or Grotewohl either was or wasn't. The 1,000 people a day, I could tell that was big — but that was it, really. And the West Germans already probably had a decent idea about that, seeing as how they were absorbing most of these people once they crossed over.

As for the other stuff, I had heard people say "but that's above my pay grade" a million times, but it really was true in my case.

"This is big," Fritz said, "very big. This is by far the most valuable stuff that Mundt has ever delivered."

"Is it big in a cosmic sense or just big in a gossipy, musical-chairs-in-the-East-German-party sense?" I said.

"Both, probably," Fritz said. "Anything where Ulbricht and Semyonov are measuring each other's dick is a big thing."

"So to speak," I said.

"Couldn't help yourself, could you?"

"We all have our purposes," I said.

"In any case, we don't know, right? Maybe it's just intramural bullshit or maybe it's bigger. Maybe they just have a staring contest and maybe the Soviets start gassing up the tanks to show the East Germans who's really the boss. Maybe it's just clock radios and maybe Ulbricht gets clocked in the fucking head. Don't know, but it almost doesn't matter. In either case, it is just the kind of information that our paymasters are hoping to receive in exchange for the checks they are writing. I need to get this out ASAP."

"Radio rather than courier?" I said. "I mean, is that even still a question anymore?"

"Yeah, it is — a little," Fritz said. We'll chance the radio for this. And it really isn't much of a chance, though. We're in the West, after all. It's not like they have those radio detection trucks like the Nazis had in Paris. They could intercept the message and crack the code, potentially. But who gives a shit, really? As long as the message doesn't include the source of the information, really, who cares if they know we have it or not? If they're about to shit-can Ulbricht and Grotewohl, we'll find out soon enough. And if they're not, well, it's just a little color, a little bit of texture added to our understanding of the relationship."

We sat for a minute longer, staring at the damn ferns. Then, after another soft whistle, Fritz was on his feet and skipping across the stepping stones in the pond.

"Come with me, old man," Fritz said, and I did my best to keep up.

8

There was a car waiting for Fritz outside the gate of the botanical garden. He told me to get in, promising me a lift to the train station later.

We drove through whatever the area was called — Berlin was so big, and this was the West, and I had no idea exactly where I was. I knew my train stop, and the way to the botanical garden, and that was about it.

It was a wealthy area, whatever it was called. Not palaces-and-polo-ponies wealthy, but more than comfortable. Secure. Solid. Nice. Like, lawyer nice. Banker nice. Business executive nice. The driver was in no discernible hurry, and I was able to appreciate the brick and the stone and the tidy lawns and the manicured gardens.

"You sure we're not being followed?" I said.

"My man Hans, it's his job to make sure I'm not. And, let me say, he's better than you."

We drove around. Five minutes. Ten minutes. There was very little of the bomb damage that you saw in East Berlin. No piles of bricks and masonry. No summer teeth. That isn't to say that there wasn't plenty of damage in West Berlin, because there was.

It's just that while the West got hammered, the East got flattened. That was the direction from which the Russians arrived, after all — from the east.

But I had seen the randomness of the thing before, in big places and small — how one block was gone and another was untouched; how one town thrived while another withered and died amid the carnage.

We passed some long, low buildings. Fritz pointed.

"American soldiers," he said. "Barracks."

"Seems like a lot of them."

"Because it is a lot of them."

"More of them than the Russians on the other side?"

"Probably not," Fritz said. "We don't have a good handle on that. We know they're in a place called Wünsdorf. It's a city that doesn't exist for Germans, unless you prepare food or clean houses or plunge toilets. Those Germans come in and out, but no others."

"A Russian city?" I said.

"A town, but yes. A Russian town. It's about a half-hour outside of East Berlin, give or take. Like I said, we know it's there but don't have anybody inside. So the numbers are only guesses. But, yes, there are a lot of them."

We drove past the American barracks, several minutes of American barracks, before arriving in Fritz's neighborhood. We swung by a cute little shopping area and a train station. The sign said the stop was called Dahlem.

A minute later, we got to the house. It was a nice little villa on a street of nice little villas.

"No bombs here, huh?" I said.

"A couple, few streets over. But only a couple."

We went inside, and Fritz poured us something out of a bottle that looked expensive. After one sip, he shouted, "Notes!" Within 10 seconds, a young guy carrying a notepad arrived.

Fritz went on to dictate a message to him containing all of the information I provided. When he was done, Fritz looked at me and asked, "Did I miss anything? Get anything wrong?"

"Nothing wrong," I said. "But you might want to emphasize the time factor. Major Asshole certainly did. He said that Semyonov wouldn't let Ulbricht and Grotewohl jack around for very long."

Fritz nodded and added a sentence to the message. Then he looked at the kid with the notebook and said, "Off you go, then."

"Send it now?"

"Right now," Fritz said, at which point the kid scampered off and we returned to our drinks.

"Where's the radio?" I said.

"Attic. Best reception up there."

"Is daytime more dangerous?"

"I think it's safer," Fritz said. "More radio traffic during business hours. It's less likely to stand out."

Fritz took another sip.

"This reminds me so much of my old house," Fritz said. "To tell you the truth, it's why I'm spending more time here and less back at HQ. You don't need this kind of hand-holding."

"You definitely could run things from Munich," I said. Fritz nodded, sipped.

"It's the same steps in the center, sitting room on the left, dining room on the right, kitchen behind it," Fritz said. "This is bigger than our house was, but very much the same. Even the runner on the staircase, that royal blue? Ours was the same color."

Nostalgia. Another part of growing old, I guessed. I really hadn't begun to feel any of that, but Fritz was more than two decades older than I was, and, well. Whatever. He was still sharp, rattling off the details to the kid taking dictation. His advice to me was always sound, and he still seemed to get a kick out of the verbal jousts. Whatever.

Fritz topped us off and then said, "I think it's time to put the heat on."

"What do you mean?"

"Your real job. The workers in the bar. I think maybe it's time to press them. Now that we know all of this stuff is going on in the background, I mean, it just screams of instability in the regime. That's what we're here to exploit, right?"

"If you say so."

"I do. And so does Gehlen back in Munich. That's why you're here. It's time to give your union friends a nudge."

"I don't even know what that means," I said. "I can encourage, but I'm not sure I can push them to do anything they don't already want to do."

"They want to do it. Union men see grievances in their sleep, even when there aren't any," Fritz said. "They're born to fight the bosses. It's in their nature — and if it wasn't, they wouldn't be union leaders."

"Except for the guy who got elected in absentia," I said, telling Fritz the story Gerd told me about being picked as shop steward at a meeting he didn't attend.

"That's bullshit, and you know it," Fritz said. "The fight, it's in their blood. And these guys, they have real grievances, not the kind that only show up in their dreams. So, a nudge."

"But..."

"And the sense I get is that they might not even need the nudge, based on what you've been saying in your reports. But, well, nudge. You'll figure out what the means when you're in the middle of it. A nudge. A little push. This seems like the time."

PART V

JUNE 6

9

The S-Bahn and then a ridiculously crowded tram took me to Müggelsee on Saturday. It was sunny and warm and, well, clearly a lot of people had the same idea I did.

Elena had told me to enter at Strandbad Müggelsee and walk to the right and along the shoreline, and she would find me. I entered with the throng and was greeted by the infrastructure of the place — bathhouses and restaurants and boat rental places and all manner of recreational whatnot. I had no idea what was here, and so I was wearing my new bathing suit beneath my trousers, with my underpants rolled up in the towel I carried under my arm. I took off my shoes and socks when I got past the last building — a place that rented those stand-up paddle boards that always seemed to me a physical impossibility — and walked down to the shoreline, slaloming between families on blankets and kids digging holes.

I looked out at the water, and it really was a nice scene — sun and sand, blue water and families frolicking. A workers' paradise, this. So far removed from the piles and bricks, and the summer teeth, and the memories that they must have provoked every day that people navigated among them.

I was fixated on two teenage boys, one on the other's shoulders, attempting to impress two nearby teenage girls, when I heard my name being shouted. That's when I turned and saw Elena. It's when I saw all of her.

Naked.

Completely naked.

Impressively naked.

I had known that nudism was a thing in East Germany, culturally accepted and all of that. And it's true, in my five minutes or so at the lake, I had seen an older woman lying in the sun without her top. But everybody else was wearing a bathing suit, and this was a first date, after all. Yet here came Elena, stark fucking naked.

"Surprise!" she said, with a squeal. When she leaned in to kiss my cheek, I had no idea what to do with my hands.

"Oh, come on now," she said.

"What do you mean?"

"My God, the shock is painted on your face — you really must be a lousy card player."

"I mean," I said. "I mean, I just..."

"Oh, shut up and follow me," Elena said, and I complied, panicked and simultaneously enjoying the view from behind, if that was possible.

After about two minutes, we crossed some invisible barrier and, suddenly, everybody was naked. Everybody except me.

"Drop 'em, old man, or people are going to think you're a pervert here for a peek," Elena said.

I looked around. It was the same mix of people as on the other side — young and old, couples and families, swimming and picnicking and digging holes. It's just that they were doing all of that while sunning their asses, among other things.

In for a dime, I thought, and then laid out my towel and stripped off my clothes.

I mean, I wasn't a prude. When I lived in Austria, people always wore bathing suits at pools and lakes, but I had been to co-ed saunas that were all naked and it seemed normal enough, I guess. But I had been there by myself or with male friends, and they were pretty much just an excuse to drink beer between sessions in the heat, and the women tended to be older and easy enough to ignore. This was different.

"What?" Elena said.

"I'm not a prude," I said, repeating what I had just worked out in my head.

"Then what?"

"I mean, it's our first date," I said. "That's different, no?"

"Only if you have a dirty mind."

I paused.

"You're thinking about that one," she said.

I paused again, then smiled.

"Let's just swim," Elena said, leading the way toward the water.

So that's what we did. We stayed in the water, and I worried about how much I likely shriveled up when we finally got out, though I didn't dare look. I don't think she did, either. Then we put on our bathing suits and went to one of the restaurants and drank some beer and ate some wurst and took in the whole scene.

"You a little more relaxed now?" Elena said, as we sat in the restaurant.

"To be honest, yes."

"Child," she said, and then she laughed. It was a nice laugh, easy, a little mocking but not quite, if that makes any sense.

"You're cute when you blush," she said, and then she laughed some more.

We took the tram and then the S-Bahn back toward home. We decided to stop in The Aerie for another drink. We were getting alone fine, but I didn't get the sense that we were headed anywhere after the bar. And, at about 7.30, two things happened: Elena told me she had to go meet a girlfriend and, just about simultaneously, her brother Gerd and his wife, Masie, arrived through the front door. Saturday night. Date night.

The women hugged, and Gerd's wife took our table while Elena gave me and her brother a peck on the cheek while we waited to buy a fresh pitcher. There was no more affection in my kiss than in Gerd's, but I still felt the day had gone fine.

The bar was full — date night — Karl was taking forever to notice us. It gave Gerd and me a chance to talk. He was the smartest of the three shop stewards, and there really wasn't a close second. He was the one who was trying to see a few moves ahead on the board, the one who was at once the most aggressive about wanting to do something about the workers' situation but also the most cognizant of what might happen if the workers pushed the party too hard. He had said the previous week at the bar, "They're fucking rats — no question at all. But when rats get cornered..."

I liked to think that we had formed a bit of a bond. I liked to think it was the smart guys' bond. The other shop stewards were good and loyal but they would always be followers. Gerd was the brains of the group, and I thought he recognized that in me as well. I could tell by the way they listened when I talked, but Gerd especially. He had no idea what my ulterior motive was. He only knew that I had a different perspective, and that it often jibed with his. I could kind of build the scaffolding upon which Gerd's emotional leadership could stand, and we both sensed it. At least, I thought so.

But that night, as we waited for Karl to fill us a pitcher, that wasn't what we talked about. It was a different topic altogether.

Or, as Gerd said, "So, you like her ass?"

I could feel my face warming, and I struggled to say something coherent.

"It's an entirely natural thing, completely innocent, unless you have other intentions," Gerd said.

I fumfered some more. Thank God it was noisy and dark and smoky.

"I mean, you didn't get hard, did you?" Gerd said.

"Uh, no, uh…"

"What, you didn't like what you saw?" he said.

"Are you going to fucking stop anytime soon?" I said.

"Probably not," Gerd said. "Certainly not as long as you keep blushing."

Not that dark, then. Not that smoky. And he wasn't kidding — he kept it up when we got back to the table. Finally, his wife made him stop. A saint that woman.

PART VI

JUNE 9

10

I had developed a routine. Late every morning, I dressed as if I were headed to an office job — which I was, allegedly. Seeing as how *Neues Deutschland* didn't publish late sports scores or, really, anything late, the work hours for most of the people there seemed to be 11-ish to 7-ish. At least, that's what I observed from the café across the street from the newspaper's front door. So, those were the hours I attempted to mimic, just in case I met somebody on the street who I knew. The odds weren't great, but it was the cautious way to play it. Besides, it got me into the shower every day and out of my pajamas, which was a plus.

Four minutes on the train from Ostbahnhof to Alexander-platz, 10 minutes on my feet after that and I was at the Babylon. I would stop for a coffee along the way, though, at one of a half-dozen places along the route. I rotated among them, just because. I mean, I couldn't think of a reason why it would be a problem that a waiter got to know me and know my order, but any familiarity on any level was best avoided. As Fritz said, when he reminded me of such things, "I mean, you are a fucking spy, after all."

The Babylon — the name in neon lights on the corner, and in a kind of up-and-down-the-stairs design on one side, with room for billboards of the movie posters above — was a beauty, I had to admit. They apparently held big movie premieres there sometimes, with the spotlights shining in the sky and the whole business. I imagined they charged big on those nights, and that's how they made their money. Maybe Friday and Saturday nights were big — I didn't know. But it was hard to believe they made enough to pay the ushers on a random midweek day at lunch. In the few days I had been there, I had seen exactly one person buying a ticket.

Anyway, I went every day to check and see if Mundt had left the signal — a chalk mark on the lamp post on Hirtenstrasse, just to the south of the theater. It turned out to be an easy place to spot an X, seeing as how the base of the lamp post was covered with what must have been decades worth of black soot that had been caked onto the metal. I mean, it can be a little awkward if you really have to stare at the thing. Imagine pretending to tie your shoe and simultaneously trying to see all four sides of the base. You can't do it and you look like an idiot if you try. Instead, you want a place where you can breeze by the thing and see the mark — and this was that, as it turned out. The X wasn't even that big, but I could still see it from 10 feet away.

Which meant I was going to Sachsenhausen, which was pushing an hour out of town. You took the train to Oranienburg — change in Lichtenberg, all in East Berlin — and then walked about 15 minutes to the camp. Except the café where I was meeting Mundt was only about seven or eight minutes. I was an hour early, just in case. I walked past the café, circled back, and poked my head in to see if Mundt was there. He wasn't, so I decided to walk the rest of the way to the camp.

As it turned out, the gates were locked and there wasn't

much to see from the outside, just some walls and fences and a lookout tower on one corner of the property. Which was just as well.

I mean, this was my third concentration camp. Mauthausen in Austria, Auschwitz-Birkenau in Poland, now Sachsenhausen. How many people had seen three of them? Himmler and who else?

My breath actually caught for a second when that realization hit me. I had heard the stories from people who had been there. I had imagined the inhumanity, lived it at least a little bit in their voices. I had seen the places they were killed — the giant quarry in Mauthausen where so many Jews had been worked to death, and what was left of the ovens in Birkenau — yet that wasn't what stuck with me the most. It was just the magnitude of the camps that I couldn't shake, the vastness of the real estate, the enormity of the evil.

I looked along the fence line at Sachsenhausen. I couldn't see the end. That was enough.

I sat on a curb for a few minutes with my back to the place, and then I walked back to the café. Mundt was sitting at an outside table, sipping something. He had ordered one for me, too.

"You went and looked," he said. A statement, not a question.

I shrugged.

"Just the outside," I said. "It was enough."

"It's closed now," he said. "The truth is, we don't know what to do with it. It's useful as a reminder of the overreach of the Nazis, the depravity of fascism, but..."

Mundt waved his hand weakly.

"Like I said, it's closed up," he said. "But we — the Stasi — we do use a couple of the buildings on the grounds for what we like to term 'special projects.'"

"But isn't it a pain in the ass to come all the way out here?" I said, and Mundt nodded.

"Hohenschönhausen — you've heard of it, the prison in Lichtenberg? No? Then again, why would you have? There are people who live a half-mile away who've never heard of it, which is how we like it. Anyway, Hohenschönhausen is easier, and really quite adequate for almost all of our needs. And their methods are highly successful. You would be impressed, I'm sure. But this is more for, shall we say, off-the-books issues. Nice and private. Out of the way."

Which I guess was why the two of us were meeting in that café. Out of the way.

"So, what am I doing here?" I said.

"Just a bit of news. Remember everything I told you?"

I nodded.

"Well, what I know now is that there was a politburo meeting—"

"And just so I understand—"

"Christ," Mundt said. "The SED is the party. The leaders of the party form a politburo. The politburo meets and makes decisions. And you have to unbutton your fly and pull out your dick before you take a piss. And B follows A and C follows B in the alphabet, and..."

"Fuck you," I said. I actually did say it that time and not just think it.

"Snappy comeback," Mundt said. "And, anyway, the politburo had a meeting to discuss the way Ulbricht and Grotewohl got undressed in Moscow, and the changes in the economic plan that Moscow is demanding."

"Yeah, and..."

"And as they were having their meeting, the feeling in the room was that they all wanted to tap the brakes, at least a little bit. To slow down, see how things settle. That was the sense of the politburo. But Semyonov — do you remember Semyonov?"

I nodded.

"Good boy," Mundt said. "Semyonov — who, you will remember, really runs things around here even if nobody says it out loud—"

"You mean Semyonov and his legions in Wünsdorf," I said.

Mundt made a face as if he was surprised — and impressed — by my knowledge of the Soviet garrison town that Fritz had told me about.

"Wünsdorf, huh? Fair play to you," he said. "Anyway, the important point is that Semyonov told them he is very much opposed to tapping the brakes. As in, not even one fucking tap. The words he apparently used were, 'Full speed ahead.' You got that? 'Full speed ahead.'"

I nodded. He offered me a ride back into the city. I told him I preferred to take the train.

PART VII

JUNE 10

11

The first fully-clothed date for Elena and I was at the Maxim Gorki Theater for a production of *Yegor Bulychev and Others*, which had been written by the man himself. Gorky. The play was a snooze, something about the revolution in 1917, and what a hellhole Russia had been before that, and what a grand spirit had developed during the revolution. Simpleton stuff.

I was much more impressed with the theater. Brand new, shiny even, small — only a couple of hundred seats — but almost like a little jewel box. Spartan, clean lines — but, still, the jewel box thing kept popping into my head.

"So, what did you think?" Elena asked when it was over.

"I like the theater a lot."

"I meant the play."

"I know what you meant."

"And?"

"I thought the play was paint-by-number propagandistic bullshit," I said.

"But what did you really think?"

I shrugged.

"Don't worry, I happen to agree with you," Elena said. She took my hand as we walked.

"Do you know, at least so far, all of the plays that they have produced here have been written by Russians?" she said. "Every one. And I've seen the program for the rest of the season — Russians, all Russians."

It was a nice night, cool. I enjoyed the feel of her hand in mine.

"Maybe a German some day," I said.

"Maybe Germany will actually run this place some day," she said.

Semyonov's name leaped into my head. I had memorized it by then, and I guess I was so proud that I needed to keep reminding myself of my vast knowledge and political sophistication. Then again, if Elena knew that the Soviets were really in charge, and I didn't find out until the previous week, what kind of idiot did that make me?

Whatever. I really didn't want to talk politics with her. This whole thing was hard enough for me, prodding her brother and his union comrades along, pushing them toward, well, who knew what? I had grown to like those guys, especially her brother Gerd, and I was already feeling bad enough that my job was essentially to put them in jeopardy — whether they wanted to be there or not. Pushing them to some kind of job action, or worse, could be the birth of all manner of unintended consequences. I had started wondering about the possibilities and requiring an extra drink at night to help me fall asleep.

Manipulating Gerd and the rest was bad enough. Manipulating Elena — well, I really didn't want to go there.

"A drink?" I said, changing the subject in a direction I might be more comfortable.

"I have a bottle at my place," she said, changing the subject in a direction where I definitely would be more comfortable.

We took the train back to the Ostbahnhof and pretty much didn't talk during the ride, the silence filled instead by the clattering of the train's wheels and the squeal of the brakes when it stopped. For whatever reason, the silence didn't seem awkward. My place was to the right of the station when you looked out the front door. Hers was straight out of the back door, a direction in which I had never walked.

After about five minutes, we came upon this massive new factory, all lit up in the night.

"What's that?" I said.

"A new plant of some kind," Elena said. "Electrical. No, heating. A heating plant — that's what it is. Gerd worked on it for a while at the very beginning. He helped pour the foundation."

It really was a massive building and so bright in the night, the cranes and other machinery casting massive shadows. They obviously were working three shifts a day to finish the thing.

"What do they need heat for?" I said. "I mean, it's such a big plant and it seems as if there are so few houses to heat."

"Other factories, I guess. That's all they build."

"So I'm not wrong, am I? I mean, I don't see any new houses being built. Like, no houses, nowhere. Just the same shitty streets."

"Shitty streets amid piles of shit."

"A poet, you are," I said.

"Shit, yes. East Germany is good at that, shit and gigantic factories. But houses for normal people? Not those palaces Gerd and his buddies are building on Stalinallee? Regular houses for regular workers, regular people? Not around here."

Elena stopped and waved as if displaying some unique grandeur.

"I mean, look around," she said.

We walked another few minutes. She still held my hand. Elena's building was on a typical street in Friedrichshain, a building bookended by piles of rubble. The apartment itself was tiny — bedroom, sitting area, kitchen, toilet, tub, all in the same room, with a curtain contraption to provide some privacy for the person sitting on the pot or taking a bath.

"Imagine my mother and father, Gerd and me, all in this one room," she said. "Parents dead now, Gerd married, only me left. You think this is shit, I know, but to have it alone? It's a palace by comparison."

The bottle we drank from was mediocre. The rest of the night was not — the rest of the night and then the morning, in the interest of complete accuracy.

PART VIII

JUNE 11

12

———

Somewhere along the way, every day — every single day — I had to find an hour or so to read that day's edition of *Neues Deutschland*. That was my cover, after all, so I had to be acquainted with everything in the paper. It was only six pages a day, so it wasn't the heaviest lift. You know, except for the colossal boredom of it all.

There was virtually no crime news, and what there was pretty much was limited to the arrest of "fraudsters" who took advantage of the common people. There was very little about sport, except as it related to the benefits to society and such. So, the staples of the popular newspapers in Vienna, for instance, were entirely absent. There were no stories about love triangles that devolved into triple shootings, no commentary about the pathetic goalkeeper with terrible hands and two left feet besides.

Instead, you got this kind of slop:

GDR HOCKEY PLAYERS SUCCESSFUL IN WEST GERMANY

GDR hockey teams returned from friendly matches in West Germany with impressive success, where numerous new friendships were formed between East and West German athletes. The most valu-

able victory was achieved by the women's team of the league team Medizin Weimar, which defeated the West German women's champions Würzburger Kickers 1-0.

That was bad enough. The rest was just mind-numbing — essentially party press releases and the like.

Controversy? Well, there was a little. The inflated price of pig heads, and a call for bringing said price more into parity with other meats, filled two columns one day. And then there was a beauty about people grumbling about a shortage of swimming caps in the winter — and how the people in charge said there really wasn't a shortage at all.

The rest, though, was like this:

A book review of this page-turner: *Walter Ulbricht: On the History of the German Workers' Movement*, Volume I.

And this attention grabber: "Marxism Wins Because It Is True."

And this fervent plea: "Save Electricity During Peak Times!"

I played a game with myself every day, a kind of challenge. I wouldn't quit reading the paper until I had come up with at least one funny tale about one of the stories and one of my fictional co-workers — a headline that had been rejected, or just some banter. On the day of the pig heads, I concocted a story about a fictional soccer game we played in the office with a ball made up of crumpled newspapers and tape, with a swimming cap on top, with the name Porky scrawled on the outside with black marker. It was stupid, but the fellows all laughed and, after all, that was the point.

I had left Elena's place in the morning and returned home for a shower and a change of clothes. It was still thinking about her, and our night, and our morning, when I stopped at a newsstand and bought that day's *Neues Deutschland*. I hadn't slept with a woman in a while, and I had been pleased with my performance. I was probably close to 20 years older than Elena, but everything worked just fine and to her satisfaction. At least, it seemed as much — and I wasn't going to spend a second wondering if it had been an act. Not one second.

I folded the paper under my arm and walked the three blocks to one of my cafés. With a coffee and a slice of rye bread and butter for fortification, I settled in and unfolded the paper.

And then I nearly knocked the bread plate off the table.

The headline:

COMMUNIQUÉ

The sub-headline:

Of the Politburo of the Central Committee of the SED of June 9, 1953

It all seemed ominous.

I thought of Mundt and the stuff he had been telling me. I thought of Fritz, too, and the radio message he had dictated. I seemed to be on the inside of history, somehow — at least that's how I felt as I started reading:

At its meeting on June 9, 1953, the Politburo of the Central Committee of the SED decided to recommend a series of measures to the Government of the German Democratic Republic which will help to bring about a definite improvement in the standard of living of all parts of the population and will strengthen security under the law in the German Democratic Republic. The Politburo of the Central Committee of the SED started from the fact that in the past a number of mistakes were made by the Party and by the Government of the German Democratic Republic, which...

I kind of zoned out for a second, unable to focus. It was as if the word "mistakes" was not in standard black type on the page but in neon. The phrase "a number of mistakes were made by the Party and by the Government of the German Democratic Republic," well, it positively screamed from the paper like the siren from an ambulance. Lights and siren, actually. I was certain that there had never been anything approaching that kind of admission printed on the pages of *Neues Deutschland* ever before.

There was some blah-blah-blah, and then this:

The interest of such sections of the population as individual farmers, retail traders, artisans and the intelligentsia were neglected. Moreover, serious mistakes were made in the implementation of the above-mentioned orders and decrees in the Bezirke, Kreise, and small towns and villages. One of the results was that numerous persons left the Republic.

Mistakes, again. Also, an admission that "numerous persons left the Republic." I mean, holy hell. Mundt hadn't been kidding. Moscow very clearly stripped Ulbricht and Grotewohl naked and demanded that they be paraded through the streets. Mistakes, twice. And people fleeing the country. All right there in black and white. To repeat: holy hell.

With that, one more:

For these reasons the Politburo of the Central Committee of the SED deems it necessary that a number of measures should be put into effect in connection with corrections in the plan for heavy industry which will correct the mistakes that were made and will improve the standard of living of the workers, farmers, intelligentsia, artisans, and the other strata of the middle class.

Mistakes, three times. I scanned the rest quickly and didn't see a fourth. Once for Ulbricht, then once for Grotewohl, and once for good measure.

I sipped my coffee. It had gone cold, and I waved to the waiter for another. I looked around the café while I waited. It was half-empty, maybe two-thirds, but every man and woman in the place had a copy of *Neues Deutschland* in front of them. None of them had turned from the front page. Some held it up to their noses and studied it. Some traced along with a finger as they read. At the next table, the guy's index finger seemed frozen in place. I couldn't see for sure, but I would have bet it was on the word "mistake."

The party in East Germany, the SED, had been all-powerful, all-knowing, all-protecting, all-nurturing, all-everything — and then, in the time it took to read a few paragraphs in the newspaper, all of that had been shot to hell. I wondered if there was ever going to be a going-back. And then, as I read the communiqué a second time — more closely the second time — I noticed something. It was something I would be able to use with Gerd and the others.

I read it a third time, just because. And then I realized that the only certainty was that I wasn't going to need a funny story when I went to The Aerie that night. There was going to be nothing funny about it, nothing at all.

13

I t was a Thursday night, but I had to go to The Aerie nonetheless. After that story in the newspaper, I had to find out — and I figured that, money be damned, they were all going to be there as if it were the weekend. And they were there, all of them.

As soon as I walked in, Hansi shouted over the din, "Alex! Alex!" He was waving his arm, waving and brandishing a copy of *Neues Deutschland*. I had never seen a copy of the paper in the bar before but as I made my way back to the table where Hansi and the rest were sitting, I saw at least three other copies laid out on different tables. All were open to the front page.

I had scooped up an empty mug at the bar and was pouring from the pitcher before I sat down. They were all, in their own way, either pointing at or staring at the newspaper as I sat down.

"Let me tell you how it went down," I said, and the three of them — Hansi, Freddy and Gerd — leaned in a little closer.

"This thing showed up on the copy desk at about 7 p.m. We already had a story in its place — something about supporting the Rosenbergs or some such shit."

"Rosenbergs?" Freddy said.

"Americans accused of spying for Russia," Gerd said.

"Doesn't matter," I said. "We shit-canned that one and put this one in its place. That's how it works sometimes when you're close to deadline. Not enough time to juggle everything, so something comes out and something else goes in its place.

"Anyway, the boss himself wrote the headline. We all read the thing — fucking mouths wide open — and tried to make sure there were no misspellings, things like that. We weren't going to edit it, though. I mean, fuck me. We weren't going to change a word. So we're doing that — proofreading with mouths wide open — while the boss wrote the headline. Like I said, he never actually did that. He would approve or disapprove the front-page headlines, but he never wrote them himself. Well, not until this one. And even after we got done, he insisted on checking the whole thing over by himself before it was sent to the composing room. And then he stayed late to make sure they didn't fuck anything up — and he never does that."

"But the headline," Gerd said. "I mean, it says nothing."

"Exactly," I said.

"How hard is that?"

"Let me tell you — he sweat bullets," I said. "He tried a half-dozen before settling on that one. Do you emphasize the message, amplify it, soften it, downplay it? Do you explain it, summarize it? Sometimes, it's obvious. Sometimes, the story is small enough that nobody will really give a shit either way. But this was big. This had to be written in such a way that my boss was not going to get a phone call in the morning. So he went with what he went with — and then he started drinking, I'm certain. My guess is, he didn't get a phone call when he woke up."

The pitcher was empty, and I grabbed it and headed over to the bar. Karl was wiping sweat from his forehead with his apron.

"The party's good for Thursday night business, it seems," I said.

"Assholes," he said. "But I'm glad they did it in the Thursday paper and not Friday."

As he poured, I rehearsed how I was going to play the next bit with the fellas. I had gone over my spiel for the rest of the afternoon, and now I just had to deliver the message. I hadn't brought a copy of the paper and was glad there was one on the table. That way, they could check.

"So, what do you think?" I said. I was looking at Hansi.

"Can't believe what fuckups they admitted to being," he said.

I looked at Freddy.

"I don't know," he said. "Like Hansi said, I guess. And they're changing the rationing, and the train fares are going down, so..."

He had nothing else. I looked at Gerd; he turned it back on me.

"What do you think?" he said.

"Me? I think they're fucking you guys," I said. When I had practiced, I thought about being subtle or direct. It was a bar. Every word was at least half-shouted. I went for direct.

"How do you mean?" Gerd said. But I could tell, just looking at him, that he knew. That he had seen what I had seen.

"They're fucking you," I said. "They don't even mention you. Artisans? Fuck artisans. Farmers. The intelligentsia? I mean, what the fuck. And this other bit."

I grabbed the paper and found the passage.

"'And the other strata of the middle class,'" I said, reading the quote. "Total, complete bullshit."

Hansi and Freddy looked vaguely confused. Gerd was different, though — head down, eyes closed, nodding.

"Why bullshit?" Hansi said.

"Why bullshit?" I said. "Where are the plumbers in their list of people who got screwed over because they made mistakes? Where are the pipefitters?"

I looked at Hansi. His face was still blank.

"Where are the glaziers?" I said.

I looked at Freddy. The message was getting through.

"Where are the concrete masons?" I said.

I looked at Gerd. He was still looking down and nodding, way ahead of me.

"Where is anybody who works at one of your job sites on the almighty fucking Stalinallee?" I said. I pointed at the paper and said, "Read it again. They're more worried about the people who left the country than the people who stayed behind to build their beautiful fucking vision of the future. Read it again. You're not in there."

I stopped, took a long drink.

"And you know what else isn't in there?" I said. "The quotas. You know, the bit where you have to work extra hard now but don't get the overtime anymore? You know, the part where they've been screwing you?"

I took another drink. I guess I had been screaming even louder than I thought because four other men — two each from adjacent tables — were now standing and listening.

"Maybe it was just a mistake that they didn't mention the quotas," Hansi said.

"Do you really believe that?" I said. "Come on, Hansi. They've been forced to eat a ton of shit here. You know that they chose every word carefully. They didn't forget the quotas. They don't give a fuck about the quotas, which means they don't give a fuck about you."

They all looked at each other, and you could see their blood rising. It was a look on their faces. It was a change in posture, as if they were all suddenly getting ready to take a swing at someone.

Freddy looked to his left and said, "Gerd?" Because he was their unofficial leader, Gerd was. They all knew he was the smartest of the three of them. Even if they had grown to trust my take on events, I wasn't one of them. Gerd was.

And he lifted his head and said, "Alex is right."

The words, just saying them out loud, seemed to change Gerd. He sat up straighter. You could see the wheels begin to turn in his head. It was as if he was back to where he needed to be. That is, the brains of the operation. They were going to count on him — for counsel, for strategy — and he knew it. And if he was as big a firebrand as any of them, deep down, I could also tell that there was a weight that he felt, the weight of responsibility borne by the leader.

I had one more thing to say, just to hammer home the point a final time. I thought about skipping it — it seemed I had accomplished what I had set out to do — but decided that one more shot of emphasis wouldn't hurt.

"I don't know what you're going to do and I'm not sure how it would all play out," I said. There were probably a dozen people standing around the table at that point, and I really was shouting.

"Like I said, I don't know," I said. "But this wasn't just some oversight. They didn't forget about you or about the quotas — they just don't care. They're more worried about the fucking people who left than they are about you, and that's just the truth. Intelligentsia, my ass. And the only way you're going to get these assholes to pay attention to you is to make them pay attention to you."

Pause. Drink.

"And they're on the back foot now — Ulbricht, Grotewohl, the lot of them," I said. "The back fucking foot. Which means, the time is now."

The shouting commenced all around me. Even Gerd was now standing and adopting a semi-confrontational posture. And with that, my work for the day was done.

14

The shouting eventually devolved into quieter conversation — quieter but animated. Lots of fingers jabbed into chests and the like. When I got up for the toilet, someone immediately took my spot at the table. I went to the bar.

"Do you have brandy?" I said when Karl finally found his way over to me. He nodded.

"Where's it from?" I said.

"Sometimes Romania, sometimes Bulgaria."

"What's the difference?"

"What's the difference between cow shit and pig shit?" he said.

Karl grabbed a bottle from the middle shelf behind the bar, held it up close to his face, and maneuvered himself beneath the only working light fixture.

"Romania," he said. "You want?"

I nodded.

"Cow shit it is," he said.

"Make it a double cow shit," I said. After my first sip, as I surveyed the scene — the intense conversations, the copies of

Neues Deutschland strewn about on the tables — I saw the door open. Elena.

"You never told me," she said. She, too, was holding a copy of the newspaper.

"I didn't..."

"You knew, right? You had just come from the office, you said."

"Yeah, I knew."

"Then why?"

"It was supposed to be a date, not a political meeting," I said.

I had not anticipated this wrinkle ahead of time. My initial instinct when Elena confronted me was to lie, to say that it all must have happened after I left the office. The problem was, I had told her brother and the rest that I had been there, and that the boss had sweated over the headline. So I just kind of blustered.

"I figured you'd find out soon enough, so what was the point?" I said.

She stared at me for about 10 seconds — narrow, angry eyes that I was afraid to engage with and, at the same time, afraid not to. But after those 10 seconds, her whole look softened. Then she smiled.

"Such a goddamned idiot," Elena said. "You know, the sex might have been better if I'd been a bit fired up."

She kissed my cheek and then left me at the bar to join her brother's table. I stayed behind, me and my double cow shit. My cover had survived, which was the most important thing. But I also had feelings for Elena, and those were also intact.

Feelings for Elena. I could hear Fritz now, if he were to find out. Whores. Only whores. I broke a lot of his rules, but none more consistently than that one. I think he knew it, too. But if he knew it this time, well, I don't know. This one seemed more important to him than most of the other operations I had worked for him and Gehlen. This one needed to be as careful and as by-the-book as I could make it. Yet there I was, getting drunk and replaying the previous night in my head. The previous night and the morning.

Still. My cover had survived. That was all that mattered as I stood there in a bar and took in the whirl. You could smell the testosterone in the place, even amid the spilled beer and the cigarette fog. Angry men. Physical men. Men who worked with their hands. Men who knew they were being taken advantage of. All men, except for Elena. And when I looked over at her brother's table, it was Elena who was holding court.

I took my drink and stood on the periphery. She was loud, and I could hear fine. I had gotten there late, but there were enough stragglers asking for a catch-up and enough lunkheads who needed to hear things three times to understand them. Between all of that and the general context, I was able to figure it out.

Elena knew people in what I guess was the East Berlin dissident labor movement, for want of a better term. How she knew them, I didn't know. But she and those people — couldn't tell how many — had been in contact since the communiqué was published. Lunch, she said. And what they told her was that there was going to be a demonstration the next day at a prison in Brandenburg-an-der-Something. The details were sketchy after that — I didn't know where Brandenburg-an-der-Something was, exactly, but I sensed it wasn't too far on the S-Bahn. Somewhere on the other side of Potsdam, it seemed. So, far but not far. Maybe an hour on the train, give or take.

Elena saw me, caught my eye for a beat and then released it, back to the group.

"This is about strength, group strength, strength in numbers, but it's also about timing," Elena said. "Now is the time. Right now."

She was picking up on the thread I had left there on the table. I looked at Gerd, and he was nodding along — more fervently than when I had said it. Maybe it was just hearing it twice. Maybe it was because it was his sister, someone he undoubtedly trusted and loved. Maybe it was because, as I had sensed, he had been thinking the same thing all along, and each repetition just provided another hammer blow of validation.

The group at the table quickly decided that they would join the prison demonstration the next day and that they would round up as many workers as they could from the various unions to join them. Someone produced a train schedule, and they did what they could to synchronize their movements.

Elena caught my eye again. She mouthed what I thought were the words, "Are you coming with us?" Then she pantomimed drawing a circle around the group.

This, I knew, was a crisis point for me. I was undercover, after all. I was an undercover agent using all of the people in that bar, using them to try to foment a reaction that, if it didn't topple the East German government, it would at least wobble it a bit.

This meant that my unspoken enemy was the Stasi. I had no idea if they knew who I was, or if I was in the country. I suspected they didn't, though, and intended to do everything I could to keep it that way. I was on the verge of something here, and the last thing I needed was to get arrested at a demonstration at a prison in Brandenburg-an-der-Something. I didn't need to be in their books, not for any reason. And, on the other hand, if they already knew who I was, I also didn't need to be spotted by the Stasi at said demonstration. Spotted, exposed, outed to the people in the bar as a foreign provocateur.

The last place I needed to be was at that prison.

Elena continued with the circle-drawing pantomime. She mouthed another word: "Well?"

And I nodded.

PART IX

JUNE 12

15

W e took an early train — the train before the first of two trains that everyone had agreed upon in the bar — because Gerd and Elena wanted to see what we were getting into before it started. The S-Bahn was half-empty and we didn't talk much — preoccupied, worried, hung over, or a combination thereof. This could end up going a few different ways, and most of those ways were somewhere between bad and disastrous. With an antsy, nervous Stasi — because their bosses were no doubt antsy and nervous — there could be arrests, or physical violence, or, well, guns. There was no way to know.

That's what I was mostly thinking about — the guns. Also, the possibility that somebody in the Stasi would be able to iden-tify me from a photograph that they did or didn't already possess. It was a long shot — that's what I kept telling myself — but it wasn't a no-shot. And if they knew who I was, and if they arrested me, it would kill the mission — and, potentially, me. But that depended on the Stasi, and their methods, and the rigor with which they employed them.

Gerd interrupted my casual musings about my worst fear — electrodes attached to a car battery on one end and my balls on the other — with the announcement, "Two more stops, I think."

"How did you get the day off — two in a row, right?" Elena said.

"First was my natural day off this week — I never get two off in a row. This morning, I called in sick for today."

"No push-back?" she said.

"None," I said. "It's almost understood that you're going to take a handful of sick days every year on the day after one of your normal days off."

"The hangovers?" Gerd said.

"Everybody understands hangovers," I said.

"My God, you do lead a soft life," he said. "I can't tell you how many times I've poured concrete hung-over. We don't get your bourgeois sick days. For us, if you don't work a day, you don't get paid. Period. So damn soft. I mean, when I was a little younger, and we really hit it hard, it was pretty common to throw up in the cement mixer when you were making the concrete. We used to swear that it set faster that way."

Our train was 15 minutes ahead of the next train, which was 15 minutes ahead of the train after that, which meant we had 15 minutes to scout out the scene before the first half of the horde arrived. It wasn't far from the train station to the prison, and when we got there, all we saw was six men outside the front gate. One of them was carrying a sign that said, "Free Harald," and that's what the six of them were chanting, over and over.

"Seriously?" I said.

"I have to admit, I thought it would be a few more than this," Elena said. "You know, from what the others said."

"And what exactly did they say?" Gerd said.

Elena took a deep breath.

"Our new best friend Harald is the head of a private hauling company," she said. "He had been arrested for some unknown reason — but the workers say it's all bullshit."

"The six workers?" Gerd said.

"They made it out like it would be more," she said.

"Are you sure you didn't just want to believe it would be more?" I said.

Elena blushed. I felt bad about embarrassing her, but the words just popped out.

"It doesn't matter," she said. "We're here now. Harald doesn't matter. We just needed an excuse, something to glom onto, and Harald is it. I wish it was more, but..."

She stopped because she heard it. We all did. It was singing, coming from the direction of the train station. And if it was just some local football team's supporters' song, it didn't matter. The first train, and the cavalry, had arrived. And hundreds — maybe more than a thousand — were in full voice. Gerd and Elena pointed them in the direction of the hearty half-dozen at the gate, and soon the singing stopped and the much louder chant began:

Free Harald... Free Harald...

We had counted on two train loads but it turned out to be six, and each was as full as the last. There must have been 5,000 people there at the peak. The crowd was more festive than ferocious, but there were some fierce moments — some rattling of the front gate, some angry shouting amid the chants.

After the arrival of the second train, the people inside the prison must have gotten nervous because that's when the Vopo and the Stasi arrived. The Vopo were quite visible but restrained — never inserting themselves between the demonstrators and the prison, merely forming a kind of perimeter line in the back. Behind them, the Stasi lurked in their black cars and black trench coats. Lurked. Watched. I did my best to keep my back to them but I really wasn't worried. They were hundreds of feet away, and nobody was picking out my face from that distance — and that was assuming that they knew my face in the first place.

After about two hours of this, I wasn't sure how it might end. Some people had already leaked away from the back, headed back to the train station.

But then the front gate opened and a man, kind of sheepishly, walked out. A great roar greeted him. They had freed Harald. The celebration that followed reminded me of the VE Day newsreels from London that I had seen back when. That wasn't my personal highlight though. That came in the middle of the thing, when the guy chanting next to me leaned over and said, "And who the fuck is Harald again?"

The train ride home — given that every other demonstrator seemed to be fortified with a flask — was a conversational riot. Three phrases dominated:

"You see?"

"Fuck them."

And, "Free Harald."

When we got back to Ostbahnhof, Gerd and the rest headed toward The Aerie but Elena peeled off in another direction. I gave her a look.

"I'm late," she said. "Gerd will tell you."

He said Elena was headed to the apartment where their 84-year-old uncle lived alone. Gerd said that the old gent's wife had died the previous year, and that he was pretty much useless in the kitchen, and that he couldn't eat sandwiches all the time. Elena went to see him once a week and made a big enough meal to provide a couple of days of leftovers. Gerd also went once a week and brought a casserole.

"Masie makes it, I presume?"

"Usually," Gerd said. "But I don't like your tone, asshole. I cook sometimes. I have one thing I make, it's called 'Pork Surprise.' Now, it's true that Masie says the surprise is ptomaine, but she's exaggerating. A case of the shits, maybe — and it only happened the one time — but not ptomaine."

The Aerie was mobbed when we got there, more crowded than I had ever seen. Karl was mobbed behind the bar. I said to Gerd, "Go to your friends," which he did, surfing through the throng. I lifted the hatch of the bar and joined Karl on the inside.

"Get the fuck out of here," he said.

"Shut the fuck up. You need the help."

"And what do you know about bartending?"

"I've worked on both side of the bar before — more time on the other side, granted, but I've earned a salary before on this side. And besides, it doesn't take an advanced degree to pour a pitcher of beer."

"But can you make a drink?"

I nodded.

"Just be sure to make them strong — that's my reputation, a generous pour, and that's what they expect at The Aerie," Karl said.

"And I won't tell them that you dilute the bottles every night after closing," I said. "You know, to balance out the generosity."

He laughed and clapped me on the back. I actually enjoyed myself for about two hours. Working the bar gave me a chance to eavesdrop on conversations from different groups, and I found pretty quickly that the tone of all of them was the same — the tone and the testosterone. I was pretty sure that a lot of wives and girlfriends were going to be awakened in the next hour or two with a nudge on the shoulder.

After those two hours, the bar had calmed down, and I needed to get out of there, and getting out with my sobriety pretty much intact was valuable. I mean, I'd had three brandies while I worked but that was it. When Karl tried to pay me, I said, "I drank my salary, thank you very much."

"That cow shit really doesn't cost me very much," he said.

"Especially after you've watered it down," I said.

He laughed and clapped me on the back again.

16

The reason my sobriety was so valuable was because my work day was just beginning. It was just past nine when I got back to my apartment. I went there for chalk. As it turned out, I had forgotten it that day in my hung-over haste to get to the train station on time, and it was by then too late to find a place to buy some, and I needed to leave a signal in the Ostbahnhof for Fritz. There was so much to tell him and it couldn't wait.

I tried to creep in quietly, and I thought I had managed, but the stairs still had their creaks and groans. When I reached the first-floor landing, the old lady who lived in the front apartment opened the door. I didn't know her name. In my head, she was always "Frau Nightgown," mostly because I had never seen her wear anything but.

"Herr Alex," she said. Half a whisper, but only half.

"Sorry to disturb," I said.

She waved her hand as if swatting a moth.

"Some bad news," she said.

I looked at her. The word caught in her throat.

"Rolf," she said.

I just stared.

"Cancer," she said, this time in a full whisper. Actually, she might just have mouthed the word.

"I've known for a while," I said. But she interrupted me with a "no... no" and two more insistent waves.

"They carried him out on a stretcher," she said.

"Was he..."

"No, he's alive," she said, "but very ill, obviously. An ambulance came — no sirens, but still. It was right around dinnertime. There were three men — two for the stretcher, one to hold an oxygen mask on Rolf's face and carry a little tank. Yeah, right around dinnertime. I had made a pork shoulder."

We chatted for a minute more. I managed to say all of the appropriate things. How I did it, I have no idea. Because even as I talked to Frau Nightgown and soothed her as best I could, all I could think in my head was, "Fuck me." Followed by, "Where the fuck am I going to live now?"

Rolf had been my savior — because he worked for the Gehlen Org, and he was the one who kept the book in our building, and because he could slide me into the vacant apartment without anyone knowing. That had been my salvation in a country where housing was the most difficult element of the spying equation.

But if Rolf died on me, so did the apartment. If Rolf departed the scene, I would have to depart, too. And the truth was, even the next day might be too late because I had no idea how close an eye the Stasi kept on its supers. My guess, though, was pretty close. My guess was that they got lists of people checking into hospitals every day, just like they got lists of people checking into hotels. Some minion somewhere would scour the lists, I was sure.

Maybe I had a day. Maybe two. Maybe.

Because once the Stasi saw that the man in charge of the

almighty book was no longer in charge — or no longer alive — a new keeper of the book would be appointed. That person would go through the records and it wouldn't take five minutes to realize that I wasn't the murdered homosexual guy who had lived in the apartment before me — and that would be that.

I needed to go, and soon. And I needed to talk to Fritz, and immediately. Fuck the chalk.

17

B ecause Fritz had taken me to the villa near the botanical garden, I knew where to find him. I had clocked the address, and had a decent sense of where it was in relation to the train station in Dahlem. Still, I walked in a circle for 20 minutes before I stumbled upon his street and another five minutes before I found the house.

There was a light on in what I thought was the dining room. I knocked softly for some reason — I mean, I was trying to wake them up, after all. A curtain ruffled and a face looked out. It was the kid with the notebook, the subordinate who had taken Fritz's dictation.

A few seconds later, the lock turned and he let me in without a word.

"You need him, I assume," he said, and I nodded. He gestured toward a small bench in the entryway, then stopped and pointed into the dining room.

"There's a bottle open on the sideboard," he said, and I didn't need to be asked twice. The kid headed up the center hall staircase with the royal blue runner, and I drank something a lot better than cow shit. Fritz arrived in about five minutes wearing a red silk robe. His hair, usually plastered down — what was left of it — was just a bit wild.

"Pour me one," he said, and I did. He took the father's chair at the end of the dining room table, the one with the arms. I sat next to him.

"You sure you weren't followed?" he said.

"Positive."

"How positive?"

"There was one drunk on my train car. He was there when I got on and he was still there, still asleep, when I got off. Asleep the whole time, snoring like a bear. And no one else got off at Dahlem. I'm sure of it."

"How about from the station?"

"Nothing," I said. "I walked in a circle for 10 minutes, just to be sure, and I didn't get a whiff of anybody."

I managed to make the wandering in a circle sound intentional, not accidental, but it was true. I really had not gotten a sense that anyone was aware of me. The streets of Dahlem were tidy and empty.

We sat for a few seconds, and then Fritz said, "Well?"

I told him about my day. When I mentioned the prison demonstration, he said, "We'd heard a little. Go through it slowly."

I did. And then Fritz said, "Going there was a risk, you know."

I explained about how the Stasi had lurked hundreds of feet away, and that I was in the middle of the big crowd.

"They have cameras, you know," he said.

"But they were..."

"Maybe cameras inside the prison — you know, maybe on the roof," Fritz said. "And dozens of junior achievers with big magnifying glasses to go over the photos, face by face."

"I hadn't thought of that."

"Clearly," he said. "But, well, it's done."

He stopped.

"Did you get all that?" he shouted.

The kid shouted back, likely from that bench in the entry-way, "Got it."

"Send it now," Fritz said.

"Just a cozy, private chat between two old colleagues," I said.

"I was just going have to repeat it to him anyway, so grow up."

"In the spy game, I'm fully grown. I'm as old as dirt."

"Well..."

"Which makes you as old as I don't know what," I said.

"Cheerful thoughts to ponder," Fritz said. He drained his glass and held it up, and I poured us both another measure.

We sipped and then Fritz said, "What do you hear from Johannes Mundt?"

"Nothing," I said.

"You have a signal set up?

I nodded.

"And you're checking it?"

"Every day," I said, which was a lie. I was probably checking it every other day at that point, but there had been nothing.

"Do you have any way to alert him?" Fritz said.

"Nope," I said. "He wanted it one-way only. But why? Is there something you need to tell him?"

"No, no, nothing like that," Fritz said. "Just wondering. If this thing is heating up like it seems to be, just wondering if he's hearing anything on his end."

I made a mental note to check the spot outside the Babylon Theater in the morning.

"There's more, though," I said.

I told him about Rolf, and about Frau Nightgown, and about the ambulance. He already knew about the cancer.

"Shit," he said. Then he just kind of stared into the distance. "I mean, shit."

"I know," I said.

"You don't know."

"I think I do."

"Maybe," Fritz said. "Maybe. The whole keeper-of-the-book thing, and the requirement to register everyone and attach them to the place where they live — I mean, it's genius. Evil genius, but still. Any Vopo on the corner can come in out of the rain, and demand to see the book, and ask a few nosy questions, and scare the shit out of everybody. And the Stasi, Christ. This is the best thing they do, and I'm not sure there's a close second."

"You've said as much before," I said. "Maybe in the exact same words."

Fritz gave me the finger in reply.

"Shit," he said. "Well, I'll start working on finding you a new place first thing in the morning. It'll probably take a couple of days, though. As long as Rolf is still among us, I'm pretty sure you'll be all right. He's still among us, right?"

"He was at dinnertime," I said.

"Do you know which hospital?"

I shrugged.

"Friedrichshain, right?"

I nodded.

Fritz leaned over, picked up the phone, and asked the operator for the number to something called the Vivantes Clinic. He dialed, waited, and asked for the nursing supervisor. Finally, he asked if Rolf Schneider was a patient.

I heard her through the receiver: "You can't speak to him at this time of night. I won't wake him."

"But he's there? What room?"

"417. Visiting hours start at 10 a.m."

"You heard?" Fritz said. "Good news in two ways. First, he's still, you know, alive. Second, he's in a regular room, not any kind of emergency or intensive care. It might mean they're just making him comfortable before the inevitable, or it might mean he's rallying. Either way, that works for us. You have at least a day or two, I would bet."

"Would you bet your money or my money?" I said.

"Only an idiot bets their own money," Fritz said. "Like I said, a day or two. I'll start looking for a new place first thing. So, I'll worry about that. You have the other business."

"Meaning?"

"You've started the ball rolling today at the prison," Fritz said. "But you have to keep pushing. You have to keep the momentum building. You can't let up, not now."

"I'm not sure I have to do anything," I said. "They're pretty fired up as it is."

"Well, just keep stoking it. Anything you can do to keep that fire burning."

PART X

JUNE 14

18

I was in The Aerie almost every night at that point, as were the rest of them. As the momentum built, as the boulder rolled downhill, it was the only way for me to keep current and to offer another little nudge here and there. That was especially true whenever there was another story in *Neues Deutschland*. Or, as in this case, two stories.

I knew it as soon as I read them that morning. The only question was how to play the obvious contradiction between them. First, I would have to point it out if they hadn't seen it, even if I was pretty sure that wouldn't be necessary. At that stage, Gerd and the rest of them were reading every page with a magnifying glass. Assuming they had seen it, I would have to provide the framing. The next nudge. It took me a little while to decide on my play, but I was happy enough after rehearsing it in my head a few times.

This was a Sunday night, usually as dead a night as there was in The Aerie. And while the place wasn't packed — Karl wouldn't need my help behind the bar — it was comfortably crowded. Like maybe a Thursday night.

Gerd pretty much jumped me as soon as I arrived at the table.

"What the fuck?" he said. "Are you people drunk down there or what?"

"Well, Schmidt does keep a bottle in his bottom drawer, and on cold nights, Winkler keeps a bottle of beer on the window ledge, and on slow nights..."

"I'm not fucking kidding."

"Neither am I."

"Page 3, Page 6 — fucking explain," Gerd said.

I made a show of picking up the paper from the table and examining both pages, even if I could pretty much recite the key parts by heart.

On Page 3, there was a series of stories related to the topic of labor productivity — and let's just say that it didn't take an advanced degree in industrial relations to know that members of a labor union wouldn't exactly be attracted to a bunch of stories about the joys of working harder.

But there was this one story. One that applauded the workers at a rail yard for fulfilling their new quotas:

FOR PROGRESSIVE STANDARDS

Technically sound labor standards are crucial for the profitability of our operations, for the fulfillment of the Five-Year Plan, and for the continuous improvement of our standard of living. The staff at Halle's freight station recognized this and committed themselves in their battle plan for strict economy to wage a constant struggle for technically sound labor and material consumption standards...

Taken as it was written, the whole thing was pretty much the kind of party-generated happy horseshit in which *Neues Deutschland* specialized, nothing more or less. Now, given how the unions and the quotas had been excluded from the communiqué, it was understandable that Gerd and the rest were more sensitive than usual to the standard happy horseshit. But, well, OK.

Page 6, though, was a different matter entirely. Because, just three pages after applauding workers who embraced the quotas, there was a story — really, an opinion column — calling for the end of the quotas.

It's Time to Put the Sledgehammer Aside was the headline.

The party organization of the nationalized housing construction industry must strive to ensure that the decisions of our Government and Party are no longer implemented dictatorially and administratively it said.

Then, later, *Mistakes were made.* But this time, they blamed it on the lower levels of the party hierarchy, not the big decision-makers at the top.

Then the story talked about "irresponsibles" who were trying *to force the building trades-men in Stalinallee to increase the work norms.*

Then, finally, in reference to the increased quotas, it said this:

A false policy which has to be brought to an end!

Yes, there was an exclamation point!

My glance at the whole thing was cursory, though. I had already seen them, and they needed to know that I had already seen them. And what I began with was, "It was some wild shit in the office."

"What do you mean?" It was Freddy, looking up from his beer.

"And hello to you, too, Freddy," I said. "What do I mean? Wild shit is what I mean. Like, total confusion. I'm just a peon there, mind you — just a copy editor. My boss is what we call the slot editor — last night, it was Jules. He sits kind of in the center of a bunch of desks arranged in a kind of semi-circle. We're the rim, the copy editors. He's the slot."

"And I'm a fucking cement mixer," Gerd said. "Just talk."

"Okay, Okay," I said. "Anyway, Jules, the slot, he's the boss when the big bosses have already gone home, like last night. And we had the bullshit about the workers in the train yard all edited and laid out on Page 3 — hell, it was there by noon, I think. But then the sledgehammer story came in — it was probably at 6 or 6.30. That's pretty late for something like that. It was messengered over from SED headquarters — they use these big blue envelopes. We see them all the time. And Jules said there was a note attached to the first page: 'MUST USE TONIGHT.' All capitals."

Anyway, I told them, Jules had no idea what to do — so he called his boss, who had left at 3.30 because he had a standing Saturday night date with a certain Eva, a redhead. Friday night for his wife, Saturday for Eva, phone call only in an emergency.

"You know," I said. "Like the night Stalin died."

I looked around at Gerd, Freddy and the rest. I had them with my practiced line of bullshit. They were completely mesmerized.

"To Jules, this seemed that big," I said. "Thank God, the boss agreed — well, kind of. When Jules told him about the 'MUST USE TONIGHT,' the boss told him about the note that was attached to the stories about the workers in the rail yard. 'MUST USE TODAY.' So, his answer ended up being, 'Use them both, and don't call me again.'"

I sat at the table and filled my mug and told them that the copy editors along the rim spent the rest of the night debating what it all meant. Did they know they were sending out conflicting messages in the same edition of the paper? Did they care?

"Eventually, I think Jules had it right," I said. "He's been around forever, seen a ton of shit go down over the years. And what he said was, 'The rail yard story, it's just the standard crap, the normal playbook. But the sledgehammer story, that's a probe. Kind of a trial balloon, maybe to gauge public reaction, maybe to gauge internal reaction.' That's the thing Jules said that seemed really smart to me. He said, 'I'm not sure they even know what they think anymore.'"

I stopped, looked at them all — face to face to face, finally stopping at Gerd.

"I think Jules is right — he really is a smart old guy," I said. "The party, they don't know what they think anymore, and I think it's time for you guys to tell them what they think. You know, tell them where they can shove their goddamned sledgehammer."

About two seconds of silence followed, and then came the explosion of finger-jabbing and fuck-thems and the rest. I knew the sledgehammer line would work.

PART XI

JUNE 15

19

Not only did I get the dead guy's apartment — I got his clothes, too. Which helped on the morning after the night before when I rummaged through the closet and found a beat-up old canvas jacket and, on the shelf, a dark gray wool cap.

I had barely slept because I was in a state of perpetual nervousness about being discovered. I couldn't shake the notion that the Stasi would come take over the book if Rolf was in the hospital for very much longer, even if Fritz had told me that I was probably good until Rolf died. Probably. Hence the on-and-off insomnia.

I knew that Rolf was still in the hospital and still alive — I had checked the previous day with the nursing supervisor at the hospital. He was more than alive, in fact. The nurse said he was improving to the point that he could accept visitors after noon if he didn't have a setback. My plan was to go see him around four. He might have a better idea about how much danger I was or wasn't in.

But first, I was going to see Otto Grotewohl, the second-highest ranking official in the East German government. Hence, the beat-up coat and wool cap.

The idea had been birthed in The Aerie the night before. My prodding and encouraging had resulted in an idea from Gerd. What if the union leaders currently employed at Stalinallee Block 40 — the construction site where Gerd, Freddy, Hansi and some others were all working — wrote up a petition calling for the revocation of the quotas? And what if they all signed it as union leaders from Stalinallee Block 40 and delivered it as a group to Grotewohl in his office?

"When?" I said.

"Now — in the morning," Gerd said.

"But you don't have the petition."

"We will after you write it."

"The hell?"

"Let's go, journalist boy," Gerd said.

"Where?"

"Believe it or not, Karl has a typewriter in his office."

"What the fuck for?" I said.

Gerd shrugged, and four of us crammed into Karl's tiny office. I wasn't really a writer or a journalist, which was a problem. The typing, though, shouldn't have been. In my previous life as a salesman for the family magnesite mine, I had developed the habit of renting a typewriter at the last hotel on my travel swing through our various clients and spending a day typing my own reports and sales orders and the like before taking the train home. I hadn't typed anything in years, but I was pretty sure it would come back to me based on the riding-a-bicycle theory of muscle memory. And it did.

The words, though. I wasn't sure about that until it hit me after I typed an opening paragraph stating, "We, the elected leaders of the blah-blah-blah unions currently employed at Stalinallee Block 40..."

"Freddy," I said. "Go get me the newspaper." Gerd looked at me.

"It's simple," I said. "Let's use their words. It's neater and cleaner, and they'll get the point immediately."

Freddy brought the paper. I identified three passages, circled them, and gave Gerd and the others a chance to digest and approve of them. When they did, I threw in a couple of whereas-es and therefore-s and pretty much transcribed the circled text verbatim. It was short, to the point, and there was plenty of room at the bottom for the signatures that Gerd would get from Freddy, Hansi, and a half-dozen others out in the bar.

I was happy with my work. The boulder really was rolling downhill now. I was going to have one more drink and get out of there when Gerd came over.

"You're coming with us, you and Elena," he said.

"No," I said.

"Non-negotiable," he said.

"No."

"What part of non-negotiable don't you understand?" Gerd said. "You and Elena are the smartest people in the circle now, and you have to be there."

"You're selling yourself a little short, buddy," I said.

"I know exactly who I am and what I am," Gerd said. "And I want you two there. I want you there to hear exactly what Grote-wohl says. There are subtleties I'm not going to catch, especially if my blood is up. I mean, there might be subtleties. So, non-negotiable."

I couldn't believe it but I agreed to meet at Stalinallee Block 40 at 11 a.m. From there, the 10 of us would walk to the party offices and demand to see Grotewohl. The risks I was taking were colossal, but I didn't see a way out. So, the plan was to dress in the old clothes that had belonged to the dead guy, stand at the back of the group, and keep my mouth shut.

When Gerd saw me, he looked me up and down and said, "Whose closet did you rob? You don't own clothes like that. I've never seen..."

"Had to look the part," I said. "And just so you know, I'm going to pull the cap down low and not say a word. I mean, if my bosses ever found out about this, I would be fired in a fucking second."

Gerd nodded.

"Thank you," he said. "Just make sure you don't shake anybody's hand."

"Why not?"

"Because you might be dressed like the rest of us, but those hands..." Gerd said, grabbing my wrist, examining, shaking his head. "Still soft as a baby's ass."

When Elena and the rest of the union heads arrived, Hansi passed around a flask for some liquid fortification, and then we walked the two miles or so to the House of Ministries on Leipziger Strasse. Nobody really said a whole lot, other than when Hansi lifted the flask about halfway there and proclaimed before passing it, "Another!" I was nervous about somehow being recognized, and the rest were uneasy about putting their names and reputations on the line. Gerd made sure to speak to everybody along the way — Elena and I could see him going from man to man, as we were walking at the back of the group. A little joke with most of them, it seemed. A little fire with a couple. But he made sure to touch them all.

"He really is a leader," I said.

"Been like that since we were little," Elena said.

"He said you were always the smartest."

"Fuck smarts," she said. "You can get smarts out of a book. But that," she said, and then she nodded toward Gerd, walking with his arm around one of the men I didn't recognize, whispering in the man's ear.

"That, you can't get out of a book," she said. "And Gerd always had it."

The first thing you noticed when you got to the House of Ministries was the huge mural that stretched the width of the ground floor. It was a massive mishmash of what must have been the artist's rendering of the ideal of East German life — people working, adults and kids playing, men and women marching beneath a banner that read "Socialism." While one of the others went in to state our case at the front desk, Elena and Gerd and I stood beneath the part where some musicians played their instruments.

"Kind of looks like you," I said.

"Yeah, me and my accordion," Elena said.

"You don't play?"

"She's not the musical type," Gerd said.

"Unlike you up there with the guitar," Elena said.

"Yeah, nice knees, by the way," I said. The guitar player was wearing shorts.

The union guy who had approached the front desk came out with a smiling woman and two unsmiling black suits. She said, "You may all come in. Please choose one person who will speak. We have 10 minutes from now."

She looked at her watch, and we followed her in. There was never a question that Gerd would be the speaker, and he had prepared a short text. We were ushered into Grotewohl's office, and I honestly thought it would be bigger. We were all jammed into the space between the desk and the door. I was in the back of the bunch, and I could almost feel one of the black suits breathing down my neck.

Grotewohl stood up and smiled, and Gerd handed him the petition. He scanned it for maybe 30 seconds and then looked back at Gerd, who read a few words that pretty much repeated what Grotewohl had already read. When he finished, the two of them just looked at each other. Five seconds, 10 seconds — that kind of silence can seem like an eternity.

"Thank you very much," the smiling woman announced, and everyone dutifully turned and filed out of the office and down the stairs and back onto the street. We were quiet and then, when the door closed behind us, we were all talking at once. What it all meant, I had no idea — but I was relieved. Even though I had to take off my hat in the office — because everyone else took off theirs — I never got the sense that anybody noticed me more than they noticed anyone else.

20

When I got to Rolf's room in the hospital, he actually looked okay, especially compared to the other two guys in the room. When I got the curtain closed around us, creating at least the illusion of privacy, he leaned over and whispered, "Did you see the sign outside the room?"

I shook my head.

"It says, 'Death's Door,'" Rolf said. Then he laughed enough that it triggered a coughing fit.

Like I said, though, he looked reasonably fit — that is, for a dying man. His color was somewhere between a little pale and deathly pallor. He was sitting up, and he'd been bathed and his hair was washed and combed. Like I said, decent.

"Good of you to come," Rolf said.

"I mean—"

"Even if you are just protecting your own ass," he said.

I dropped my eyes. I think I blushed.

"I'm kidding — it's not like we're really friends, or family, or anything."

"Brothers of a sort," I said.

Rolf smiled.

"Brothers in treachery," he said.

"You've watched my back, and I promise you, I'll be watching yours," I said.

"It'll be a short-lived task for both of us, then," Rolf said.

I wasn't sure how to reply. Nobody was good at these kinds of conversations, other than maybe priests, and I certainly wasn't a priest even if I had impersonated one a few times in my undercover work. Anyway, Rolf jumped into the silence.

"I'm not coming home," he said.

I stammered.

"Don't," he said. "I've made my peace."

"But—"

"Shut up," Rolf said. "Like I said. I'm at peace. And on the way to my next place, nothing will make me happier than knowing I've helped you get to your next place."

Pause. Rolf laughed.

"Different places, certainly," he said.

"From your lips."

"But you know how you can help me?" he said. "I know it breaks every protocol there is, but if you could give me an idea what you're up to, I don't know. It would add to my happiness. And to my peace."

It did break every protocol there was. Volumes of protocols, in truth. Compartmentalization of information was everything in my business. Compartmentalization, need-to-know, all of that. My mind immediately drifted to my worst fear, the electrodes attached to my balls, and to the certain knowledge that I would blab everything I knew before my inquisitor had time to shock my nads for a second time. That's why you didn't tell your comrades any more than was absolutely necessary.

But Rolf was dying. He had days, maybe a couple of weeks, and no more. There really wasn't anything the Stasi could to do him, I didn't think. So, protocols be damned. I told him anyway, told him everything, told him about Gerd and Elena, The Aerie and Grotewohl's office. I told him and I saw him smile in a way that I never had.

But then his face returned to normal.

"Shit," he said. "I almost forgot."

"Almost forgot what?"

Rolf then told me about his last day in the apartment — maybe six hours before the ambulance came.

"I would have left you a note..."

"On the blue paper."

"I think I got a sheet out of the drawer before I passed out. It might still be on the floor."

Rolf's eyes kind of glazed over. He yawned. The nurse had told me, "Ten minutes, no more," and I was pretty sure my time was about up, and she didn't seem to be the sort who could be cajoled into an extension.

"What happened, Rolf," I said.

"A guy with a badge happened."

"Where?"

"My front door."

"Not the regular Vopo?"

Rolf shook his head.

"Not Vopo at all?"

Another shake.

"And he asked for me by name."

"Yes, Alex, by name."

"Shit."

"Indeed, shit," Rolf said. "I played dumb, which isn't that hard for me. I said I didn't know you, had never heard of you, didn't recognize the name Alex Kovacs at all. Anyway, he asked to see the book, and he flipped through it, and then he left. I wasn't able to even get off the couch at that point, and I was in and out of it, but I'm pretty sure I heard him go up the stairs toward your place. But, like I said, I was pretty out of it. It could have been a dream, I guess. Maybe, maybe not."

"Fuck."

"Indeed," Rolf said. "Have you been back?"

I told him that I had slept there the last three nights — that I had been worried about the Stasi and the book, but that I figured I was okay.

"As long as—"

"As long as I was still alive?" Rolf said.

I nodded. Again, I think I blushed.

"But—"

"Shut up," he said. "Just business. And I think you were smart. I mean, you didn't know about the man with the badge, which means that staying there was actually stupid and surviving for three nights was lucky. But you didn't know, so... They'll have somebody in my place within 48 hours after I die, but not likely before. The trigger will be the death certificate. I'm convinced that the East German bureaucracy is fueled by printed forms, and nothing else moves the machinery of government. So, you were right. I think you're good until the nurse down the hall fills in the form that probably already has my name typed on the top."

"Except for the man with the badge who knew my name," I said.

"Exactly."

"Which means—"

"You can't go back to the apartment, Alex," Rolf said.

Pause. Difficult breath.

"You can't go back for one reason, I can't for another reason," he said.

Another difficult breath.

"But never is never all the same," Rolf said.

21

M y intention was to go to Elena's, given that I couldn't go back to the apartment. I just couldn't chance it. I figured my boyish charm, and a bottle, would earn me a night at her place. After that, I had no idea.

The problem was, Elena wasn't there. So I left the bottle on the doormat and went to The Aerie. And, as it turned out, Elena was there along with pretty much everybody I had ever met in Berlin.

The scene was wild. If there was such a thing as electricity in the air, it would have been a fire hazard — well, more than the usual fire hazard. Big crowd, lots of noise, a hundred conversations. Fingers pointed, shouted declarations, half of them bouncing up and down on the balls of their feet. So fired up.

And then I saw Gerd. No shout, no bounce. Calm amid the storm.

At the bar, I caught Karl's eye, asked if he needed help. He shook his head. "Besides," he said, "I think you're needed over there."

He motioned toward Gerd.

"What for?"

"Don't play dumb," he said.

"Not playing, brother."

"The fuck you're not," Karl said, and then he turned to a customer on the other side of the bar. What exactly that meant — *the fuck you're not* — was unclear to me. If he thought I was a trusted advisor to Gerd, that was one thing. If he thought that I was manipulating Gerd, that was another thing entirely. How he might have reached any conclusion, other than by his powers of observation from behind the bar, was also a mystery. I walked away and chose to believe in the trusted-advisor scenario. Anything else would be too complicated.

As it was, I pretty much ran over Hansi when I turned away from the bar, what with my head so far up my own ass and everything. He gave me a proper hug after the impromptu one, and told me what was going on. He said that there had been a group decision to return to the House of Ministries in the morning, but this time in big numbers.

"Hundreds for sure, but I bet thousands," Hansi said.

"No shit?"

"Absolutely no shit," he said. The alcohol had turned "absolutely" into a five-syllable word, though. Five, maybe six.

I saw Gerd again. Calm. Grim. And then I saw Elena, standing on a table in the opposite corner of the room, standing and having trouble maintaining her balance, standing and stomping to the point where I was sure the table would collapse. Standing, stomping, and leading a chant:

Fuck the quota...

Fuck the quota...

Fuck the quota...

I walked toward Gerd. He was staring at Elena when I reached him. I put my arm around his shoulder, rested it there, and pointed at his sister with my other hand and leaned into his ear and said, "So what else besides dancing doesn't run in your family?"

He didn't laugh.

"You heard, right?" he said.

"Hansi says hundreds, maybe thousands."

"This time, Hansi is not full of shit," Gerd said.

"Thousands," I said, and then I whistled in admiration.

"I guess," he said.

I had only a few seconds to come up with a reply. I wasn't sure because I wasn't sure why Gerd was so clearly worried. If it was just that the movement was getting away from him, and that he maybe was a control freak and couldn't abide not being the wise man in charge, that was one thing. But if he sensed imminent danger — that is, a reaction from the Stasi or maybe the army — that was a different matter entirely. The one thing was just a matter of his pride. The second, though, was more serious. It was the definition of what I had been sent to Berlin to encourage — a challenge to the East German party and its authority. Because of that, I had to downplay the consequences to Gerd.

And then he said, "Shouldn't we wait?"

"For what?"

"To give Grotewohl a minute."

"You've heard the phrase, 'Strike when the iron is hot'? Well, it is sizzling, my friend. Look around. Sizzling."

He panned the room and so did I. And while I wouldn't admit it to him, I could see why he was concerned. These guys really were out of control, and it was clear, when he looked at me, that Gerd wanted me to admit that I saw it, too. I really did want to tell him, too, but I couldn't. I couldn't and I wouldn't. The mission, after all. I couldn't and I wouldn't.

So I told him, "It's smart to move now. The door is ajar. It's begging to be kicked open. In a way, I think the party might be begging for it, too. Just think about that editorial in the paper. They were testing it out, removing the quotas. They want to do it. Now, you guys can give them a reason. Really, think about it. They're dying for a reason, and here you are."

Gerd listened closely — me talking into his ear amid the din. As I backed away to take a drink from my mug, I looked at his face. It maybe softened, just the tiniest bit.

"But there's something else," I said, back in his ear. "I told you why I think it's the right thing, but let's talk about you now."

"Fuck me," he said.

"Listen, asshole," I said, and I got even closer to his ear. "They need you today, and tomorrow, and the day after. They fucking need you — and your sister, if she doesn't kill herself on that fucking table."

"So, what's your point?"

"My point is, this is a crucial moment. The pot is about to boil over. The lid hasn't blown, but we both can see it happening. You have to manage that. And the thing is, though, that if you tell them they can't go tomorrow, well, you tell them that and you'll lose them. They won't listen to you anymore. They'll mock you, call you a pussy. You know it as well as I do. And then where are you? Nowhere."

I stopped, drank.

"That can't happen," I said. "Because they're going to fucking need you more tomorrow than they do today, and even more than that a month from now. If this works like you hope, and the unions end up having some kind of working relationship with the party in the future, it needs to be you at the negotiating table."

Stop. Drink.

"It needs to be you," I said.

Gerd didn't say anything in reply. I told him I would see him in the morning, and left him standing there, arms folded, scowling amid the maelstrom. And in the far corner, Elena, joined now by Hansi on the tabletop, was stomping and chanting:

Fuck the quota...
Fuck the quota...
Fuck the quota...

———————

22

There was one light on in Fritz's house, in the front room. I could see his assistant, or whatever the kid was, through an opening in the curtains. He was reading the newspaper, sitting in a big, comfortable chair. I chose to rap softly rather than use the big brass knocker, and the kid heard me just fine.

"Really?" he said.

"Just get him."

He looked at his watch.

"It's that important?" the kid said.

"Would I be dragging my ass all the way out here if it wasn't?" I said.

"Fine. You know where everything is," he said. He turned toward the stairs and pointed without looking back at the dining room where I had talked to Fritz before, the room with the sideboard and the expensive bottles. I was into my second pour — admittedly, I drained the first glass in two gulps — when Fritz arrived in the same red silk robe.

"Over here," he said, and then he walked into the room

where his boy had been sitting when I arrived. Fritz plopped into the comfortable chair, leaving me with a stiff little settee.

"Well?" he said.

And so I began a five-minute ramble, getting Fritz up to date on everything that had happened and about what was about to happen, as well. He shook his head when I told him about accompanying Gerd and the rest to Grotewohl's office.

"Reckless," he said.

"Nothing happened."

"That you know of. All right, keep going."

I told him about the scene in The Aerie, about the undeniable fire that I felt when I was there among the working men. And I told him about the march on the House of Ministries that was scheduled for the morning.

"How many?" Fritz said.

"Probably thousands."

"Good, good," he said. Then the old man rubbed his hands together, like somebody who had just hit big at the blackjack table in Monte Carlo.

"I guess, but I don't know for sure," I said.

"Oh, for fuck's sake. Get yourself another drink and get me one, too."

I walked across the hall to the dining room and filled two glasses as instructed. In the entrance hall, Fritz's assistant was sitting on a wooden bench, reading his newspaper again.

After I handed Fritz his glass, and we'd both taken a sip, he said, "You do realize that you are on the verge of a great success here. Like, a perfect success. Not a slip-up, not a deviation. It's like it was drawn up in a textbook. It never happens that way — as you know as well as anybody — but it's happening here. It's all falling into place, and quicker than either of us imagined. You should be thrilled."

"And yet," I said, and then I took another sip.

"This is the mission," Fritz said.

"I know."

"Don't tell me they're your friends now."

I didn't answer.

"This is the mission," he said, again.

"And if someone gets hurt?"

"What part of 'this is the mission' don't you understand?"

"But what if—"

"We want what if," Fritz said. "We want it all — chaos, violence, whatever unpredictable outcome you can imagine. And you knew that back in Vienna when we plotted out the whole scheme."

"I know, but—"

"No fucking buts," Fritz said. "You're not a kid, for God's sake."

I drank. He drank. And then Fritz shouted in the direction of the entrance hall.

"You heard, right?"

The assistant walked the three steps toward the doorway, showed himself, and nodded.

"Get the message out immediately," Fritz said.

The kid turned to leave, but Fritz stopped him.

"You can get word to my friend at RIAS, can't you? Even this late?"

The kid nodded.

"A meeting in the morning — early," Fritz said.

When we were alone, I asked Fritz, "What's RIAS?"

"Radio in the American Sector."

"And we give a fuck about them because..."

"They can be helpful," Fritz said. "They transmit from the American sector but they have a lot of listeners in the East. A lot. They can be very helpful, and you're going to explain the situation to them, and then they're going to figure out what to do with the information."

"Why me?"

"Because I said so," Fritz said.

He walked across the room, opened a closet door, and reached for a pillow and a blanket. He tossed them on the couch on the other side of the room.

"Anything from Johannes Mundt?" he said.

I shook my head.

"You even check for a signal?"

"Not like I've had a shitload of free time," I said.

"Yeah, yeah, whatever," Fritz said. "We almost certainly know more than he does at this point — you know, except for the Stasi's response. But, fuck it. If you fall asleep quick, you might get six hours. And you're going to need them, I would imagine. Long day ahead."

PART XII

JUNE 16

23

The kid woke me at six, pointed to a bathroom down the hall, and said, "I'll be in the car. Fifteen minutes tops, but 10 would be better." I took about 20 minutes, probably. He was reading another newspaper when I arrived. He started the engine as soon as my door slammed and drove away from the curb. For maybe five minutes, neither of us said anything until I finally cracked.

"Do you have a name?"

"As far as you're concerned, no," he said.

"For fuck's sake."

"You do this for a living, right? I mean, this isn't your first time, right? But even a virgin knows about compart—"

"Compartmentalization," I said. "Fuck me. It's not like I asked you for a hand job."

After a pause and a grimace, he said, "Call me Max." And then he said, "And just for the record, if anybody's giving out hand jobs in this relationship, it's going to be you."

"Smart-ass. Okay, now I like you," I said.

We drove for a few minutes. Quiet streets. On the Ku'damm, the neon at the movie palaces and the nightclubs was turned off.

I tried to remember if I had seen any neon in the East. I tried but I couldn't recall any. The lights and the marquee at the Babylon were bright enough, but neon? I didn't think so.

"So, who is this guy we're meeting?" I said.

"Dieter Hartmann. He runs RIAS."

"And why are we talking to him? I mean, shouldn't we be talking to the CIA, and then they would talk to Herr Hartmann? That would seem to be the protocol."

"Yeah, about that," Max said. "The main reason we're going direct to Hartmann is that General Ritter—"

"He hasn't been 'General Ritter' for a long time. He's just fucking Fritz to me."

"I thought it was 'Uncle Fritz,'" Max said.

"Smart-ass."

"I try," he said. "But seriously — I know you're close to him, and I know it goes way back. But anyway, Unc and Hartmann go back even farther, back to when they were both in army cadet school."

I whistled.

"Eighteen ninety something."

"Eighteen eighty something, I'm pretty sure," Max said. "The way he told it to me was, 'I shoveled the horseshit, and Dieter dumped the wheelbarrow into the pit.' So, that's part of it."

"Only part?"

"The rest is politics, economics, commerce — take your pick. But the Gehlen Organization gets paid for delivering information to the US, and if we followed your protocol, well, Unc is concerned that the CIA would take the credit and, as he said, 'Gehlen would be left with his dick in his hand, not a money order from Harry Truman.' So."

"It's not like they get paid by the tip, though, is it?" I said. "I mean, it's not like the success or failure of one operation makes the check bigger or smaller, right?"

"Yeah, you're right," Max said. "At least, I think you're right. It's an ongoing relationship, and I guess relationships have ups and down. But if it was a line on a graph, you still want it going up and to the right. This is the kind of thing that would do that, help keep the line going up and to the right."

"You pick up on all this just by reading the papers and sitting on that bench in the entrance hall?" I said.

"No, he actually talks to me to my face when you're not around."

We drove some more through a city just shaking off the cobwebs. It was so close to the East but so different. Cars for one. You needed to give up either a firstborn or a left testicle to get a car in East Berlin, and they were all beat-up shit-boxes. At 6.30 in the morning in East Berlin, all you saw on the streets were people trudging toward the S-Bahn. In the West, though, we were stopped at a light behind a convertible. Blue. Chevrolet.

Cars. Neon. All explained by the accident of geography, but not like how the city on the deep side of the river develops faster and richer than the town on the shallow side because you need deep water to build a port. No, not that kind of geography. This was man-made geography. Actually, more like cartography.

"There's one more thing," Max said. "I'm sure you can handle it, but be prepared for Hartmann to be pissed off."

"And why is that?"

"Because he's expecting to see Fritz at the meeting, not his wayward fucking nephew."

"Christ," I said. "So why isn't Fritz coming?"

"You might not have noticed, but he's not a kid anymore. He doesn't do early and he doesn't do late. He's dynamite at lunchtime, though. Fucking gangbusters."

I didn't say anything. Neither did Max. He turned into a side street and parked outside a café whose lights spilled onto the still-dark pavement.

"Don't get me wrong," he said. "I love the old man. Maybe not as much as you. That's probably impossible — I've only been working for him for a year and a half. But I do love him."

Pause.

"But he is old," Max said.

I opened the car door, but Max didn't move.

"Come on," I said.

"Nope," he said. "Hartmann might be pissed at you, but he won't tolerate me. I'm just the hired help."

24

The café was empty except for a single man sitting at the table in the deepest back corner. His face was hidden behind a newspaper. I approached his table and stood there. He either never sensed my presence or was playing some kind of power game. Two, three, four seconds went by.

"Well?"

The newspaper never moved.

Power game. Asshole.

"I'll talk to you when you put down the fucking newspaper," I said.

Two seconds. Three.

The paper came down.

"Where's Fritz?" Hartmann said.

"Thanks, I will join you," I said.

He stared. I stared back. He twirled a loose hair in his left eyebrow. Both brows looked like matching birds' nests, gray and brown and bushy and tangled. Then Hartmann raised his hand to get the attention of the waiter and pointed at the place in front of where I sat. Another coffee.

The waiter was quick. I took a sip before I finally explained myself.

"Fritz sent me," I said.

"Why?"

"Because I know the information better than he does," I said.

"What information is that?"

"Do you want to take notes?"

"I'll just listen," Hartmann said.

And so I told him — not everything, just what had happened in the last day or so. The delegation from Stalinallee 40. The petition. The quick history of what had been printed in *Neues Deutschland*. The meeting in Grotewohl's office. The decision to march on the House of Ministries that morning to demand the end of the work quotas.

Hartmann listened intently. He stopped me.

"How big a march?" he said.

"Hundreds to thousands — likely thousands," I said.

"From all of the unions?"

I nodded. He waved for more coffee.

"Bread and butter?"

I nodded. I couldn't remember the last time I had eaten. He told the waiter.

"And you work for Fritz?"

"In a manner of speaking."

"And you're in on this?"

"Close enough," I said.

Hartmann whistled softly. The bread and the coffee came. I inhaled the two slices. Hartmann just watched me. He waved for the waiter again.

"Petey, I know the kitchen isn't really open yet, but you must have a couple of hard boiled eggs in the cooler, no?"

Petey nodded, looked at me. I held up two fingers. He was

back quickly enough, and I inhaled the two eggs, too, stopping only to salt them between bites.

My mouth was still half-full with the last of it when I said, "So what happens now?"

"Depends on you, my friend," Hartmann said.

"What do you mean?"

"We can't invent something out of thin air," he said. "We're a radio station. We report the news. We don't make it up. We can't make it up. You need credibility with your listeners. Fiction would just drive them away. So, like I said, it depends on you."

"To create some nonfiction," I said.

"Exactly."

"But, well, come on. You're not getting a heads-up on a union demonstration from your old pal Fritz — your brother in shit-shoveling back at cadet school—"

"He told you that?" Hartmann said, laughing.

I nodded. Max told me but, well, same thing.

"The point is, he didn't send me here to give you advance information on this whole thing just so you'd be in a position to report on it accurately. I mean, am I right?"

Hartmann sipped at his coffee. He'd eaten nothing.

"It's like this," he said. "We can't make it up, like I said. It has to really happen. There's no question about that. But if it does happen — if you and hundreds-to-thousands of your new best friends do march on the House of Ministries and demand an end to the work quotas — then we can help. We can amplify. Even if the leaders of the march are sane and sober, somebody in the group will not be. Threats will be made, things like that. And like I said, we can amplify the parts that work best from our perspective."

Then, without a goodbye, he dropped a few coins on the table and left.

25

I t was just after 9 a.m. when I arrived at Stalinallee 40. Max dropped me off a few blocks away, and I walked the last bit. The noise built with each step I took toward the building site. It wasn't yelling, nothing like that. It was more of a buzz, an undercurrent, and it just got louder and louder.

I'm pretty lousy at crowd estimates but I looked around and did a few calculations and a bit of mental math and concluded that there were more than a thousand men gathered at the construction site — plus one woman, Elena. She was standing near a big truck that seemed as if it was going to be the focus of what was next. She was there, beaming, and Gerd was next to her. He was holding a bullhorn at his side.

A thousand men. More. And there was one other thing I noticed: easily half of them were holding a liquor bottle of some sort. Not beer — the hard stuff. If you've ever been in a train station, you've seen people drink in the bars early in the morning before they got on one of the long haul expresses. So, 9 a.m. wasn't unheard of. Still, though.

A guy stood on the back of the flatbed — I didn't recognize him — and Gerd handed him the bullhorn. What followed was a short speech that easily must have broken the world record for "fuck thems" in a 60-second stretch. He jumped down, and the next guy jumped up, and it wasn't much more subtle. The reply from the crowd of men with the bottles was an echoing "fuck them." There were a few "fuck Grotewohls," but only a few. When I heard the first one, I reflexively looked around to see if I could spot a Stasi uniform, or a black trench coat, or something. But I didn't see anybody. It was just the union men, and their bottles, and their grievances.

Finally, it was Gerd's turn to climb onto the back of the flatbed. He was the closer, I imagined. He caught my eye just before he raised the bullhorn to his mouth and squeezed the trigger thing that turned it on. A quick look. I couldn't tell if it was meant to say anything more than hello.

Gerd's speech was the best by far — impassioned but literate. Thoughtful. A here's-why-we're-here-today kind of thing, and they listened. Most held their liquor bottles at their sides. Gerd really was good at this.

And then he caught my eye again, right before his peroration. And I thought I knew what he was saying then. I thought he meant to tell me that he had heard me, and that he needed to find a way to lead this mob, to corral it, while at the same time encouraging it.

And so, after he looked at me, Gerd said:

"This is the day, my friends. This is the day we show them — the ministers, the party, all of them. Am I right?"

They all cheered, many raising their bottles.

Gerd continued:

"We march as one — that is how we show them. We speak as one, and as loudly as we can. We claim our rights. We demand change. We do it peacefully, though. We do it peacefully but we do it as one — and there is no strength greater than men united. We attack no one — only their ideas, starting with the quotas.

We hurt no one — only their pride. We destroy nothing, other than their belief that we will just continue to roll over and take it."

Now Gerd raised his left arm and pumped it as punctuation while holding the bullhorn with this right.

"Today," he said.

Pump. Cheer.

"A new day," he said.

Pump. Louder cheer.

"A new dawn," he said.

Pump. Louder.

"To the ministry."

Pump. Louder.

"To get what we deserve."

Pump. Louder.

"To get justice," he said.

Pump. The loudest roar.

And then Gerd hopped down from the back of the flatbed and began to march down Stalinallee toward the House of Ministries. Hansi and some others were with him at the very front, and Elena and I weren't far behind. The hundreds and hundreds and hundreds followed behind.

It was more than a mile to the House of Ministries, the first bit of the journey on Stalinallee. Half of the construction in the country must have been in various stages of completion along the massive showpiece boulevard. Passing other sites, the marchers shouted for workers to drop their tools and join them. Some did. Most probably didn't, but a decent number entered the line of march.

I looked around. It was orderly enough, I guessed, given that it was a drunken mob. There was some coarse chanting — you know, like, "Piss on the party" — and the occasional car that honked in an attempt to get through the procession found itself shaken by a dozen marchers, but there was nothing crazy or particularly dangerous along the route. At least, not that I could see.

Elena and I barely talked as we walked. Wherever our relationship had been headed, well, let's just say that it had veered off course. The reality was, it never had a chance to stay on course, not as long as I was hiding my little secret about being an undercover agent using her and her brother and the rest of them to kindle and encourage what amounted to an insurrection against the East German government. Given that, there wasn't going to be much of a long-term potential. Still, I did like her, and I was attracted to her, and I thought the feeling was mutual. Now, though, this whole thing had taken over her entire person.

We were walking, and I was looking around, and I guess my face showed the endless calculating and analyzing that I was doing, and she said, "You don't feel it, do you?"

"I don't know what I feel. I mean, it's overwhelming."

"It's inspiring," Elena said. "It's exhilarating. I'm tingling. It's like sex but it's better somehow."

"Better than with me?" I said, reaching for a laugh line. Elena just shook her head, though, and turned to look forward again at Gerd and the others. Then she turned and looked back at the massive crowd behind us, and then up at her brother again. She was glowing — there was no other way to describe it. She couldn't wipe the look off her face if she tried, a look of joy and wonder and determination, all somehow melded together.

26

W hen we had been there before, only the day before
— could it have been only the day before? — the
House of Ministries looked like any other office
building, albeit one with a big socialist mural along the ground
floor. It was just normal, a regular office building with regular
people bustling in and out, doing what I presumed to be regular
business things. Suits and briefcases and hurrying. We had all
seen it a million times. Anybody who had ever spent time in a
big city had.

But this was not typical. That was obvious.

The claustrophobia began to hit me as the marchers
crowded into the plaza outside the building. It still seemed like
more than a thousand people, and that was even acknowledging
the group that had broken off from the main parade and
decided to make themselves heard outside of party headquarters on Wilhelm-Pieck-Strasse.

Many had joined during the march — not only union
workers but also a sound truck with speakers much louder than
Gerd's bullhorn. The message from the truck was a "down with
the quotas" mantra, repeated relentlessly. Gerd didn't react to it

as we walked but even Elena, after 10 minutes, said, "Christ, don't they have a flip side?"

As we packed into the plaza, Gerd hopped onto the back to the flatbed and was about to try to get everyone's attention with the bullhorn, but the sound truck was like a bazooka compared to his popgun. So he hopped back down.

"What do you think?" I said.

"We're about to fucking find out," Gerd said.

A guy climbed onto the back of the sound truck.

"Who?"

"From the hospital site, I think," Gerd said. Further down Stalinallee, a massive construction site was to be the future home of Friedrichshain Hospital.

The guy started speaking, and it was all reasonable enough — cheering on the workers, denouncing the quotas, things like that.

But then:

"And I tell you right now, my union brothers. This is our moment! Look around you. This is our time! We will never be stronger! And we will never get what we truly deserve — we will never show the men in that building what we are all about — unless we got on strike as one!"

I looked at Gerd. He looked worried.

"A general strike," the man on the sound truck shouted. And all around us the marchers crammed into the plaza turned toward the House of Ministries and pumped their fists and chanted in unison, "Strike! Strike! Strike!"

Amid the din, Elena leaned over and whispered something to Gerd. He replied with a shrug. He looked at me and I mouthed the words, "General strike?" Again, he shrugged.

The crowd remained back from the building, although there were bulges in the line here and there. There was one security guard on the door, only one. He didn't look nervous, at least from what I could see, which made him either a wonderful actor or brain dead. Out of the crowd, two men approached the guard and said something to him. He turned and went inside.

"Shouldn't that be you?" I said. I was then standing next to Gerd.

"Out of my hands, it appears," he said.

"Since when?"

"Since somewhere along the route, it appears," he said. Another shrug.

When the security guard went inside, the sound truck started up again.

"They asked to see Ulbricht," came the voice on the loud speaker. The crowd booed.

"They asked to see Grotewohl." More boos. Neither was popular but Grotewohl seemed to be hated more for some reason, even though he was only the second in command.

A minute or so later, the security guard came back out of the front door and returned to his post. At ease, looking unconcerned, even as the boos rained down on him.

Maybe five minutes later, two men emerged from the front door, one of them holding his own bullhorn. The crowd didn't take but a few seconds to realize that they were two nobodies, neither Ulbricht nor Grotewohl. They were much younger and looked nothing like the photos in the newspapers.

The one guy began talking, but he was tough to understand. Somehow, the House of Ministries had a lousier bullhorn than the union men.

I strained to follow what the guy was saying but was able to catch snippets. I did hear him say, quite clearly, the words "studying the quota issue." I also was pretty sure I heard him say, "your patience is appreciated as," but I could make out anything after that. The people in front, though — the ones closest to the lousy bullhorn — were booing the speaker mercilessly. When he was done talking, he and his compatriot and the lousy bull-horn fled back into the building. The security guard, amid the torrent of boos, remained placid.

Word began to filter back from the people in front. It was, admittedly, a ragged game of telephone, but the consensus seemed to be that the guy with the lousy bullhorn promised to return with more information. That meant we were all staying — except for the steady procession of people who left to find a place to piss or buy another bottle before returning. After a while, the singing and the chanting and the speeches became tedious, but the crowd was just about as big two hours later than it had been at the start.

Then the front door opened. A man came out — a different man, not one of the earlier non-entities. He wasn't Ulbricht or Grotewohl, but he did have a better bullhorn than the first guy. He spoke slowly and was easy to follow.

And what he said, and then repeated, was this:

"After consideration by the party, the work quotas are being eliminated, effective immediately."

I heard it once, and then the second time, and turned to hug Elena — except she was already hugging her brother. The two of them were jumping up and down as they hugged, and then Gerd said, "We won. We fucking won."

The problem was, almost nobody else was celebrating. There was no great roar of approval from the crowd. Some applause, yes, but it was not from a majority of the crowd. Not even a healthy minority, if I was being honest. After maybe 30 more seconds, the guy with the better bullhorn was being drowned out by boos and shouting. As he gave up and retreated back into the House of Ministries, the shouting unified into a new chant.

"We want free elections...

"We want free elections..."

As the whole thing broke up — it was past lunchtime at that point and the liquor bottles had been drained, after all — that was the chant that echoed through the streets as the thousand or so departed in knots of dozens.

"We want free elections...

"We want free elections..."

Gerd, Elena and I walked to The Aerie in a kind of shock. At one point, Gerd said, "We won, and then somebody changed the game without telling us."

"It never came up? Free elections?" I said.

"Never," Gerd said. "Right?"

He looked at his sister.

"Never," Elena said.

The bar was pretty full by the time we got there. Every once in a while, starting with the pipefitters, the chant would go up and pretty much everybody in the place would pick it up. Even Elena, at least half-heartedly.

"We want free elections...

"We want free elections..."

Gerd and I took a pitcher and sat in the farthest corner, away from most of the shouting. He was stricken.

"We fucking won," he said. "No more quotas. We won. It's enough for now. It's time to digest this whole thing. I mean, think about it. We have a new relationship with the party. For the first time ever, the unions have demonstrated their strength — and we have real economic gains to show for it. Everybody in this place just got a raise in pay this afternoon — a real fucking raise. I kind of think we need to settle down now."

He looked at me.

"You agree, right?"

"I guess," I said. "You did win. And I would have thought that would have strengthened your position."

"Like, me personally?" Gerd said. "I guess I did, too. But

that's fucking gone. This is totally out of my hands now. I'm clearly not in charge."

"And who is?"

"Fuck if I know," he said.

"And how did it get away?"

"Same answer," Gerd said. "All I know is they were listening to me when we left Stalinallee 40 and I was an afterthought by the time we got to the House of Ministries."

"And all it took was a sound truck," I said.

"And someone to yell into its microphone," Gerd said. "Although I never heard him yell anything about free elections — well, not until after the guy came out of the building and told us that we had won."

Sometime around the third or fourth pitcher, word reached us in the back corner of another demonstration scheduled for the morning. It was set for 7 a.m. at Strausberger Platz, and it would be followed by another march on the House of Ministries.

"Gonna be huge," Hansi said after clapping Gerd on the back. Huge was a three syllable word at that point. Maybe four.

Gerd looked beyond worried, and I understood. I also sympathized, even though I shouldn't have. Chaos had always been the goal of the mission, and this promised to be chaos multiplied several times over. I was winning. It was all working. And yet, well, Gerd had become my friend. And the concern on his face was what I felt.

In the middle of the fifth pitcher, Elena swooped by and grabbed me and dragged me out of The Aerie without a word. A woman in heat. We kissed on the street outside the bar, and I was pretty sure she would have dropped her knickers in the alley if I had asked.

Instead, we walked the few blocks to her place in double-time. It was a warm night, and a lot of windows were open, and from many of the apartments, a newscast about the demonstration at the House of Ministries was playing. They did a station identification, and it was RIAS. Radio in the American Sector.

Suddenly, I recognized a voice. It was Hartmann, Fritz's old partner in shoveling horseshit. And what he said was, "The call for free elections was loud and persistent at the demonstration. The clear perception among the demonstrators was that the party is vulnerable, and that all that would be required to break down the door would be one persistent shove. Given the way that the party conceded on the quota issue, it is hard to argue with that logic. One persistent shove really might be all that it takes."

It was about then that the coin dropped for me. I wondered if Hartmann had somehow supplied the sound truck. I wondered if he had actually written the script that the guy was reading.

I wondered all of that for another two blocks, and then we were inside Elena's apartment, and most every thought somehow became secondary to the matters at hand.

PART XIII

JUNE 17

27

"Where are we going?" I said.

"Brandenburg Gate, if I had to guess," Gerd said.

"But why? The House of Ministries," I said, pointing off to my left.

"We're passengers at this point," Gerd said. "And you, when you don't own the railroad, all you can do sometimes is hop on the caboose and ride."

Elena and I had picked up Gerd at his apartment at 6.30. I was exhausted, Elena elated, Gerd seemingly resigned. We arrived at Strausberger Platz at 6.45, and the crowd was easily five times bigger than the one from the previous day.

Gerd took a 360-degree turn and did his own calculation.

"Ten times bigger," he said.

And the thing was, it just grew over the next hour — 20,000 people, maybe 25,000. Men came from every direction and, by my own scientific count, only about one out of four was carrying a liquor bottle this time instead of half. So, something.

In the distance, I could hear at least three sound trucks that must have been at least a quarter-mile away. All of them began to tell people to head for the House of Ministries, and then we were all moving as one, a giant, amorphous snake headed west down the middle of Stalinallee.

Because it was so much bigger than the day before, every-thing was just *more*. In some cases, that meant more chaotic — more bumping into each other, more spilling over onto the side-walk and knocking over trash barrels and such. In other cases, it meant more organized. There was the squadron of sound trucks, for one thing. For another, a small percentage of the marchers carried signs that someone had supplied. Two of the common ones said "Down with the government" and "Butter, not arms."

More chaotic, more organized — and, sometimes, more outrageous. Political posters, many featuring the photos of party bigwigs, were pulled down and set on fire. One guy shimmied himself up a lamp post to pull a poster down and, to massive cheers from marchers passing by, dropped his pants, squatted, and took a dump on Ulbricht's face. He was drunk but had decent aim, all things considered.

Gerd was walking between Elena and me. She was off to the right, beaming, just aglow, and not because of my efforts the previous night. I was to Gerd's left and he was neither beaming nor aglow. He was, I don't know, not catatonic but just mystified.

"I know some of this is organic," he said. "I mean, it gets big enough and it just grows on its own. It's like this march — you just get carried along by the whole momentum of the thing. But somebody has to be in charge somewhere. I mean, the sound trucks. The change in messaging from yesterday morning to the afternoon. It was the quotas, and then it was free elections, and now it's those signs: 'Down with the government.' Where does that come from? Somebody had to print them up. Where?"

He paused, looked around.

"Who?" he said.

I had an idea that I couldn't possibly share with him — that some combination of my boss and his brother in cadet school horseshit-shoveling had more to do with what was going on than I ever could have imagined. But as I thought about it, well, what the fuck? I could broach the theory.

"Who?" I said. "Did you listen to RIAS last night? Have you thought that, I don't know, maybe..."

Gerd looked at me, deep into my eyes. I mean, not so deep that he could see the truth about me, I didn't think. But deep.

"It's all I could think about last night," he said. "I mean, I barely slept for a hundred reasons, but that was probably number one. They have this deep-voiced announcer and I just kept hearing him: 'This is Radio in the American Sector with the latest news.' They just kept stirring it up. The free elections business was just, like, I don't know, repeating on a loop. Nothing about the quotas — almost nothing. Free elections and Strausberger Platz in the morning, then Strausberger Platz and free elections — on and on and on."

He looked angry at that point, not as mystified. It was as if it all seemed truer to him now that it wasn't just an idea in his head, that he was saying it out loud.

"What if they're using us to fuck with the party?" he said. "I mean, what if we're just a bunch of useful idiots? Yeah, I've thought about it a lot."

For some reason, we both turned to the right at looked at Elena — maybe just because we were both worried about losing her in the mob. She was chanting with some people nearby — "Free elections... free elections..." — and she was just so enlivened by the whole things. Chanting and enchanted.

I grabbed Gerd's shoulder.

"Useful idiots? That's bullshit," I said. "Don't ever fucking say that again. You had a legitimate cause that you were fighting for. Those quotas were killing your men, and you got them changed.

That was a real, major accomplishment. Don't ever forget that. Real. Life-changing."

"Yeah, for about five seconds," he said.

He looked around again at the incomprehensible mass of humanity that we were a part of, all of us trudging westward.

"Five seconds," Gerd said. "Like a fart in the wind."

He had been correct about where we were headed. In the distance, we could see the Brandenburg Gate and, 15 minutes later, we were there. The House of Ministries was off to the left, not that far away, but for some reason we went this way. As we got closer, Gerd and I noticed two things simultaneously — that there were no guards at the gate and that a man was charging inside to climb the interior steps. A man who looked suspiciously like...

"Fucking Hansi," Gerd said.

Maybe 30 seconds later, Hansi emerged at the top, sprinted over to the flag pole in the center, and took down the East German flag. It took him a minute to unhook it from the lines after he lowered it, but after he did, he tossed the flag down into the crowd to a great roar, and then to a nice little bonfire.

Another roar.

"Fucking Hansi," Gerd said, more to himself that time than to me.

28

By 9 a.m., maybe 9.30, there must have been 25,000 people crammed into the plaza in front of the House of Ministries. The difference between that morning and the previous morning could not have been more stark – the difference between a ragged rabble and an overwhelming mob. People were jammed in close enough that new claustrophobics were being created by the hundreds.

The sound trucks were far enough away — stuck on side streets, unable to advance anywhere near the plaza — that you really couldn't make out what they were saying over the ambient crowd noise. Two guys had bullhorns, and they were closer than the sound trucks, but they also were so much weaker that the result was the same.

The mob was on its own, swaying this way, oozing that way, entertained only by the chant that grew and then ebbed:

"We want free elections...

"We want free elections..."

At a certain point — 10 minutes, 15 minutes after we had arrived — Gerd poked me in the ribs and gestured toward the House of Ministries.

"Did you notice?" he said.

I turned, looked.

"Not until just now," I said.

Just as the crowd had grown by a factor of 20, so had the security presence guarding the front door of the building. The one placid guy posted at the entrance had been replaced by maybe 100. I didn't know who they were — Vopo, Stasi, or likely some combination.

"Not armed, though," I said.

Gerd patted his armpit and said, "Maybe there."

"Doesn't make much sense."

"Why?"

"If they're supposed to be a deterrent, a few guys very visibly toting rifles would be more effective, I would think," I said. "No, I don't think they're armed. They're counting on numbers being the deterrent, not weapons."

"They think 50 or 100 against this mob would scare anybody?" Gerd said.

"They've been scaring people with a lot less for a long time," I said.

Just then, a surge in the crowd carried all of us about three feet to the left. I looked to my right to see what the source of the push was but I couldn't tell. All I saw were people, thousands of people, filling the plaza and spilling onto the side streets that fed into it.

"So, now what happens?" I said.

"Nothing good, I'm afraid," Gerd said.

Some time after 10, the crowd — whether by boredom or by some invisible design — became more rambunctious. Specifically, the line of men at the very front of the crowd — the ones facing up against the front door and the big socialist mural — began to surge and then recede, forward and back, forward and back.

They never made contact with the legion of security men, who were perched a couple of steps above the mob. I was lasered on the scene, and I saw the Gerd was, too. Most of the people around us didn't seem to be paying attention, absorbed in their conversations and their whatnot, but Gerd and I were entirely focused.

Surge and recede. Surge and recede. Gesturing from the men in front and tightening of the ranks of the security cops. Surge and recede. Surge and recede.

Then, sometime after 10 o'clock, the latest surge did not recede. The mob was going for the door — and, within about 10 seconds, everybody in the crowd saw what was happening and the roar grew with the emotions.

The security guards tightened even more, and I saw one of two of them swinging what must have been batons of some kind at the protesters. No guns, though. And while they put up a good fight for a few minutes, the dozens were no match for the thousands. And the truth was, for every baton I saw being swung by a security guard, I saw at least two liquor bottles being swung in return.

After five minutes, maybe, the last of the guards were beaten. The only thing preventing the mob from opening the door was the surge of their cheering brethren behind them.

It took a few seconds — 20 or 30 — to get the crowd back enough to pull open the door. But I didn't see what happened after that.

Gunfire will get your attention that way. Gunfire and tanks with red star decals on the sides, well, even more.

If you can scan into the distance while ducking, I did it. The tanks were coming from at least three different directions — tanks and big vehicles out of which armed soldiers were bounding. There clearly had been planning, and the front door must have been the trigger. For some reason, and for a second or two, the thing I thought about was Major Mundt, Major Asshole, passing along the intelligence about Ulbricht and Grotewohl getting their asses handed to them in Moscow.

After the first shots, the panic was entirely predictable. Given where we were, closer to the House of Ministries than to the back of the plaza, Gerd, Elena and I were pretty much trapped with nowhere to go. So we stayed low, the three of us, Gerd cowering over Elena to protect her and me doing my best to shield them both.

After a minute, maybe two — time became impossible to calculate amid the shooting and the confusion — enough people had gotten away from us that I was trying to figure which direction made the most sense for us to run. But before I had decided, there was a burst of gunfire and, about 20 feet away from the three of us, a man fell.

Gerd got up.

"Wait, do you know him?" I said.

"Doesn't matter — come on," he said.

The two of us crab-walked over to the fallen protestor — younger than us, a good-looking kid. The bullet had gotten him in the leg, and he was bleeding a lot.

"Come on," Gerd said. He grabbed the guy by one armpit and I took the other and we dragged him — but where? Which way was safest? We had no idea and so, unspoken, we chose a direction at random and just kept dragging.

We were doing okay, and so was the guy. He would need a tourniquet on that leg, and soon, but he was still conscious and if we could keep him that way for another 150 feet or so, there were some parked cars we might be able to perch behind and get a belt tightened around that leg.

A hundred and fifty feet.

Bang.

Another shot. Close.

And then Gerd dropped his armpit.

And then Gerd groaned.

The bullet entered his chest. If it didn't hit his heart, it didn't miss by much. The blood didn't spurt out as much as it oozed. His dark blue shirt was now stained black, and the stain was growing.

I sat him up, one arm behind his shoulders, but that didn't make a lot of sense. So, instead, I made a pillow out of my jacket and rested his head on that.

I looked around for an ambulance or something with a Red Cross on it. All I could see though were the tanks and the vehicles with the red star decals on the sides.

"Stick with me, buddy," I said, because that was the thing you said, even if you had no idea what to do.

Gerd smiled.

"Yeah, buddy," he said.

I kept looking around, hoping against hope. Next to us, the good-looking young kid had passed out. His face had gone completely pale. Maybe we had been kidding ourselves when we started trying to drag him to safety. The truth was, I had been ready to leave him from the start. It was Gerd who insisted.

I looked down at him. Scarily pale. He seemed to be trying to say something, and I leaned down close to his face.

"Useful idiots," he said.

I sat him up again, holding him by the shoulders.

"That's bullshit and you know it," I said. We had already had the same conversation, but he needed to hear it again. I looked at him, and his eyes were open. He had heard.

Five seconds. Ten seconds. Eyes still open and blinking.

"Maybe," he said, and then he gasped.

"Maybe," Gerd said, and then he died in my arms.

Even though it was obvious that I was going to have to leave him there, I still couldn't let him go. It seemed like forever when

I finally did. The trigger might have been Elena's screams. She was about 50 feet away, separated from us in the confusion, but not so separated. She obviously had seen everything.

Fifty feet. Sixty feet. A hundred feet. And then, still screaming, she was being shoved into the back of some kind of military vehicle by two soldiers. They had red star decals on their helmets.

29

I looked around, trying to figure out what might be next. Other than the realization that I would never forget the date June 17, 1953, or the sight of Gerd's eyes closing as I held him, I had no other thoughts.

I looked down at my shirt — no blood. I couldn't believe it. By all rights, I should have been swimming in it. But the wound to Gerd's chest hadn't gushed, and I had held him from behind, and, well, whatever. I was clean except for a small blood stain on the back of my right hand. I spit on it and then rubbed the hand on the inside of my pocket. Gone.

I thought, just for a second, of trying to follow the wagon that was driving away with Elena inside. I was pretty sure I had seen a dent on the back left fender, and that would give me something. But as I scanned the plaza, I saw that it was impossible. In the chaos — the tanks, and the shooting, and now some smoke — I just couldn't keep track of the vehicle, dented fender or no dented fender, and wouldn't have been able to reach it if I had. And, well, then what? What if I had caught up with it? I wasn't armed and was prohibitively outnumbered by the soldiers with the red star decals on their helmets. I mean, then what? Talk about the dog catching the car.

I looked down at Gerd. I looked at the good-looking kid, poked him, put my ear down near his lips and mouth to try to hear a breath. Dead also.

And with that simultaneous realization — Elena gone in the back of a wagon, Gerd and the kid dead — the survival instinct kicked in. I scampered behind the row of parked cars that I thought might give me cover to put on the tourniquet. Several of the car windows were shot out, but I felt relatively safe for a few seconds. I raised my head high enough to do another quick survey and just made a decision: north. Up Wilhelmstrasse.

Rather than crab-walk, I chose to run as fast as I could. Two blocks would probably be enough. Along the way, I heard one shot that might have been intended for me. It pierced the plate glass of a dress shop I was running past instead of me, though. And that was it. Soon, I was walking at a relatively normal speed in the middle of downtown Berlin, just another man on the street.

Not that there were a ton of people outside at that point. There were Vopo on every street corner, though, and they were strongly encouraging people to get off the streets. As in, "Get the fuck home, sir." I waved and pointed, as if that was my intention, and they let me go. They weren't arresting anybody, not that far away from the House of Ministries.

With that, I knew I needed to get to Fritz, which meant I needed to get a train at Friedrichstrasse Station.

It was about a 15 minute walk. Maybe 20, but more like 15 because I wasn't dawdling. And in between waves and points at the insistent Vopo — "Gotta get to Friedrichstrasse for the train," I shouted, over and over — I couldn't help but wallow in what I had done.

I would think of Gerd in my arms. And I would remember

Fritz saying, "This is the mission." I would come very close to convincing myself that the whole thing was bound to happen anyway, that my little nudges at the beginning were nothing more than that. In my worst moments, though, I would think about a little nudge that propelled a snowball down the hill, a snowball that grew bigger and bigger and traveled faster and faster until it crashed into something at the bottom, destructive and out of control. All from a little nudge.

Eventually, I settled on different analogy — maybe because it was true and maybe because it just made me feel better. Anyway, I wasn't starting an avalanche. Instead, I was just like the bumpers in a bowling alley — that's what I had been. Just keeping things on track. Just making sure that the whole thing didn't veer off course. But that's all I was. Just guardrails. Because they were still going to roll the ball themselves, with or without me. And the pins were still going to get scattered, whether I had been at their table all those nights at The Aerie or not.

I liked that one better, and it was true, too. Mostly.

Mostly.

Friedrichstrasse Station was crowded, as always, but maybe even a little more chaotic despite the presence of dozens of Vopo — or, maybe, because of their presence. I headed toward the track where the S1 train to Wannsee left — Fritz's house was on that line — but was stopped at the top of the steps by two guards.

"Not running today, sir," they said.

"Why not?"

"No trains running that cross over into the West today, sir. Only trains that stay in the East are running. Now, please move along, sir."

And that pretty much settled that. Instead, I took a train East to the Ostbahnhof. There, I left Fritz the customary chalk signal, seeking a meeting. What good it would do with the border between East and West closed to train travel, I had no idea. Maybe it was open to cars.

I left the mark, and looked down at the piece of chalk for some reason before shoving it back into my pocket. There was a dot on it, reddish black. Gerd's blood, from when I had wiped my hand inside my pocket.

My first instinct was to toss the chalk into a dustbin, but I kept it. I wasn't sure why, but I kept it and I played with it as I walked to The Aerie.

30

I had seen The Aerie empty and quiet, and I had seen it full and raucous. I had never seen it full and quiet, though. Not until that night — the night that Gerd died.

Hansi had seen it all, as it turned out. He was openly bawling at the table. He hugged me, wiped his tears and his snot on my shoulder.

"You guys were trying to save that poor fucking kid, weren't you?" he said.

"It was Gerd's idea, not mine," I said.

"I'm sure," Hansi said, and then he began crying again, and then he stopped suddenly.

"Elena?" he asked.

"Arrested."

"By who?"

"Beats the fuck out of me," I said. "I think the Soviet soldiers, but I don't really fucking know. It was all such chaos out there. I mean, you saw."

"But she wasn't shot?"

"Not that I saw, Hansi," I said. He clapped me on the

shoulder and left to give a table of other people I didn't recognize the news.

I walked over to the bar, and Karl poured me a tumbler full of some rocket fuel without asking. He was crying, too. This really was a wake.

"Anybody — you know, among the regulars — besides Gerd?" I said.

"Two of the steamfitters. That's all we know for sure. Young kids. You know…"

He stopped. His breath caught.

"You know, those loud assholes," Karl said, and then he started bawling, turned on his heel, and refilled somebody else's pitcher. In a few minutes, though, he was back.

"Don't you have to work?"

"Fuck work," I said.

"But so much news."

"You're joking, right?"

"They can't ignore this."

"Watch them." I said. "I'll go in later, after a drink. But you'll see. They'll have some happy horseshit on the front page about a bumper crop of cucumbers, or some such nonsense."

"They can't totally ignore it," Karl said.

"They'll try. And if there is anything, it'll be on the inside pages somewhere. And don't think for a minute that they're going to admit that the Soviet tanks had to bail out their asses. Don't even pretend to believe that they'll mention that Khrushchev was fucking Ulbricht's wife while he and Grotewohl stood there watching."

"But it's all over RIAS — they're repeating the story every 15 minutes. Everybody has heard," Karl said.

"Well, guess what?" I said. "I guarantee you that in the next two days, tops, the party will put out some kind of statement that RIAS is bullshit fictional Western propaganda, and that good and loyal East Germans should stop listening to it immediately."

"Yeah, but..."

"You'll see," I said.

I had no idea what was in the first tumbler, or the second, but I was well along at that point. And that's when it hit me: this was going to be my last visit to The Aerie. Gerd's wake was going to be it.

For some reason, I had never imagined what the end would be like. Most times, I would be on some kind of mission and spend the final days knowing it was about to end and plotting my escape out of the country. That's not what I was doing here, though. I was just a quick S-Bahn ride away from where I needed to get, provided they opened up the westbound trains again. In that sense, I'd had nothing to plot.

I had been thinking less about the end than the process. I guess I just figured that the end would come somehow and that would be that. And the thing was, the end was undefined. If it had ended with the quotas being lifted, there was a chance Fritz would have declared victory and gotten me out of there. As it was, he was certainly going to get me out now. But even though I knew it was possible, I never really anticipated what had happened in the plaza outside of the House of Ministries. Elena, Gerd — no, I never imagined.

And now, I was never going to know what happened to Elena. I was not going to be able to pay my respects to Gerd. Karl poured me another short one, and I was wobbling, when it all hit me.

And Fritz's voice was in my ear: *"Don't tell me they're your friends now."*

Interrupting my stream of consciousness, Hansi came back to the bar. He seemed as drunk as I was. He wasn't crying anymore.

"You really saw her go, right?" he said.

"Elena? Yes," I said.

"Any guesses?" Hansi said.

"Any guesses about what?"

"Any guesses about where they took her?"

"I told you, I really don't know," I said. "It could be a dozen places. A hundred places. How many Vopo stations are there in a city like this? How many Stasi offices? And then there are the Russians. I mean, I have no idea if they have their own jails, or how they deal with their problems. Talk about needles in haystacks. It's just... I don't know. Impossible."

We talked some more. I asked if someone had told Gerd's wife, and he said Freddy and a couple of the others did it — Freddy's wife apparently was a good friend of Gerd's wife. I asked about Gerd's body, and Hansi shrugged. We figured that would be the wife's burden now, finding him to bury him. Christ.

31

I needed to sleep, which meant I needed a place to sleep. It had crossed my mind to try Elena's apartment but that seemed something beyond crass. Besides, I would have to break down the door and hope that nobody else in the building heard me. Besides that, how would I explain myself if one of her concerned friends showed up looking for her?

So, I did a calculation as I stood on the sidewalk outside The Aerie. Common sense told me that with everything that had gone on at the House of Ministries — with the Vopo out on the street corners and the Stasi undoubtedly occupied with interrogations of those arrested — the notion that they were worried enough to bother with my apartment seemed far-fetched. So, I would sleep there. One more night, after which I would find a way to get to Fritz, the first step toward getting me back home to Vienna.

When I arrived at the building, I saw the front room on the first floor was lit up. The super's apartment. Was Rolf back from the hospital? Or had Rolf already been replaced?

I opened the front door as quietly as I could and crept up the stairs, avoiding the third step from the bottom, the squeakiest step. At the first landing, I knocked on the door and the old lady opened it immediately. It was as if she was waiting for me.

"Rolf?" I said.

"This afternoon," she said.

She saw the confusion on my face and said, "He died this afternoon. That's his brother downstairs, cleaning out the apartment. He said it was peaceful."

"So quick?"

"The Stasi man told him it had to be empty by noon tomorrow," she said.

I thanked her and started walking up the stairs but she said, "Wait." Twenty seconds later, she reappeared with two shot glasses filled to the brim with something that, as it turned out, was disgustingly sweet.

"To Rolf," she said.

Anyway, I had one night. The way I figured it, the trains would probably be running again to the West in about 48 hours, but I really could only chance the one night in the apartment. So, I would sleep, wake up, and then try to find a way to cross over to the West on foot or by car. For all I knew, it would be as simple as crossing the street from Mitte into Wedding. I thought I might be able to do that anywhere along Bernauer Strasse, from the Russian sector to the French. At least, I thought it was the French. And there was no way they could block the whole street. There weren't enough Vopo on the force.

Anyway, that would be for the morning.

I fished the apartment key out of my pocket and unlocked the door. I didn't see the note — I stepped on it and slipped, the envelope skidding me along the linoleum and straining my groin in the process. It took me a few seconds to get to my feet, curse, massage myself, find the light switch, and then get the envelope open.

It was a short note:

Be at the off-the-books place tomorrow at 6 p.m. Go to the main gate. Wait there and I'll find you. And don't even think about not coming. That girlfriend of yours will be there, and her life depends on your attendance.

The note wasn't signed.

It didn't have to be.

PART XIV

JUNE 18

32

             ―――――――

If Fritz had been in charge of my life at that point, I know what he would have said: "Run!" Actually, "Fucking run!"

If the unwritten rules and regulations of espionage in foreign countries were being followed, I know what I would have done: found a way into West Berlin, across Bernauer Strasse or likely a hundred other places, and been done with it. With East Berlin. With Elena. With everything. Mission accomplished and straight back to Vienna.

Because, honestly, what did I think I was going to be accomplishing by meeting Major Mundt at Sachsenhausen? What kind of Superman did I think I was going to turn into? He was a Stasi major, and likely was supplied with Stasi resources, and I was me — unarmed and unprepared. Did I really think I was going to be able to save Elena from his evil clutches, like some hero in a silent movie? What was I going to do, fight off Major Asshole with my bare hands and then untie Elena from the railroad tracks before the onrushing train severed her in two? A variation of that was playing in my head, but honestly.

It was, objectively, madness — unless I was willing to trade myself for Elena, and then trust that Mundt would keep his end of the bargain and let her go. In other words, trust the guy who was blackmailing me. The notion was absurd on its face.

Objectively, madness. And yet, there I was, checking the S-Bahn route map in the station to plot a way to get to Sachsenhausen on an East-only train. The announcements in the Ostbahnhof were being repeated about every three minutes: no westbound trains until further notice. Sachsenhausen was in the East, but the most direct train cut through the West for a bit. It only took a minute to figure out an alternative. I had to go deeper into the East a few stops to Lichtenberg and then change trains for Oranienburg. Simple.

The trip was easy, as it turned out, and the trains were busy. End of a normal workday in the socialist paradise, it seemed.

As I rode the two trains, and then walked from the station to the Sachsenhausen camp, all of the same shit kept flying through my mind. That Gerd and Elena were grown adults who had made their own decisions. That I hadn't forced them to do anything. That I had only encouraged them. That I had just been the bumpers keeping the ball in the alley. That I had nothing to do with the Soviets bringing in the soldiers and the tanks. That I was just the bumpers at the bowling alley. (I tended to repeat that one a lot.)

Now, though, since I slipped on the note in the entryway to my apartment — former apartment — there was one more line of thought added to the maelstrom: Mundt. He had been known to Fritz and me and the rest as a Stasi major who was feeding information to the Gehlen Org. Most of the information fell into the realm of color about the major players in the East German party. That is, nothing earth-shattering, but it was valuable nonetheless. Intelligence work was a lot like the creation of a mosaic, and the tiles Mundt had been supplying added highlights and shadows. They made their overall image appear to be more real, more life-like.

But, well, now what?

He obviously knew who I was and what I had been up to. He knew where I had lived — he was probably the guy who Rolf told me about earlier, the guy who wasn't Vopo and who had asked for me by name before flipping through the book. He knew all of that, and he knew that I had slept with Elena. Which meant he knew everything. He likely knew my shoe size at that point.

So, what had he been doing? Protecting himself somehow if the Gehlen connection was discovered? You know, "I was secretly penetrating their organization. I gave them nothing of value, and now I can supply you with names and addresses, et cetera." A smart insurance policy, honestly. So it might have been that, or it might have just been a Stasi officer with the means to scratch an itch of curiosity and maybe gather a morsel that he could leverage for more money from Gehlen. Those were the only two things that made sense to me. It wasn't as if he was working to sabotage my attempt to incite a workers' insurrection — because, well, he had to know what I was doing and allowed it all to take place anyway.

The café where I had met Mundt the last time was doing a lively after-work business, but I didn't see him at any of the tables on the patio. I kept walking and arrived at the main gate to the camp about 10 minutes before six. There was no one there and nowhere to sit, so I plopped down on the curb and tried to think of what I might be able to trade for Elena — you know, short of me. Maybe some Gehlen information — structure of the organization, a few names, something like that. Maybe I could pledge myself as a double agent, just as Mundt had done, except I would inform the Stasi about what the Gehlen people in East Germany were up to. Maybe I could invent a crumb or two to start. Maybe something about Max, the kid who was working for Fritz. The car. I could tell about his car, and maybe pretend he was a courier of sorts.

I was making the thing up as I sat there, trying out ideas and then discarding them as quickly as they had flown into my brain. I sat there, head in hands, when a car drove up and braked about three feet from me.

"Get in," Mundt said. His lackey opened the gate and drove us into the camp.

33

W e sat in an office — Mundt behind the desk, me in a club chair. It was pretty comfortable. I could imagine a luscious Nazi secretary in a tight Nazi skit sitting there and taking dictation from the flat slob who ran the concentration camp. I could hear him asking questions for her to research.

How many bodies compared to last month?

How much hair was collected in July?

How much did the gold from the fillings weigh?

I kind of shivered at the notion. Then I looked at Mundt, sitting there with a pistol in his lap, and shivered again.

"Are you wearing the homosexual's clothes, too?" he said.

He really did know everything.

"Same size, just about," I said.

"I can't believe..."

"Can't believe what?"

"That you have such low standards," Mundt said.

"Well, I associated with you," I said.

"Said the man whose fate is currently in my hands," he said.

I just stared at him. I mean, he wasn't lying. I needed to curb the smart-assery. Then again, it might not matter at all in the end, and if the ship was going down, I might as well enjoy the orchestra.

"I'll save the explanation for later," he said. "So, let's just get down to it. I need you to agree to confess to espionage and to encouraging the insurrection that took place this morning outside the House of Ministries. In other words, I need you to confess to the truth. In exchange for that confession — again, to the truth — your girlfriend will be set free."

As I had expected. I would be a feather in his fucking Stasi cap, and that was the price for Elena's freedom.

"Define 'set free,'" I said.

"I don't know, set free. Free to leave. Free to go."

"And free to be arrested again as soon as she gets three blocks away from this fucking nightmare of a place?"

"No," Mundt said. "Hardly. Free is free. But I can't guarantee how that will look in a few days. Things are a bit in flux at the moment, as you might appreciate. I mean, you created the flux."

"Hardly," I said.

"Whatever," Mundt said. "All depends on where you're sitting, I guess. Anyway, we were talking about flux. Disorganization. Chaos. Systems stretched beyond their normal limits. Officers working 18-hour shifts. The point is, I can guarantee her freedom until our little piece of the world calms down. After that, and after the paperwork gets properly arranged, she is less likely to be an unnoticed loose end. Capisce? So I would strongly suggest that the lovely Elena — and she is lovely, as I'm sure you're aware — make her way across town to West Berlin in the next, I don't know, 36 hours."

"So that's it?" I said. "Get out of jail free for the next day and a half? With nothing but the clothes on her back and maybe a knapsack?"

"It ain't nothing," Mundt said. "It's a lot more than you're getting, you might have noticed."

As he spoke, I did my best to reconnoiter my situation without looking like it. So I glanced around the room as subtly as I could. It was just an office — a big office — with an open door in the back right corner, an open door leading who-knew-where. The desktop was empty, which meant there was no paperweight or pencil sharpener or coffee cup for me to grab and throw at Mundt.

Then there was the pistol. I tried not to stare but I think I probably did. He held it in his lap as he leaned back in the desk chair. More fondled than held, it looked like. His finger was not on the trigger, though. Flaccid, then, as it were.

"So, how long have you known?" I said. I figured I would play for time, although I wasn't sure what I was hoping might happen if I delayed the inevitable by five or 10 minutes.

"Known what?" Mundt said.

"You know. About... my recent work endeavors."

"A little while. Saw your apartment. Shithole."

"But about the rest of it?"

"The rest of it?" Mundt said. "Meaning the part where you are a foreign agent working to bring down the government of East Germany? Working to bring down the government by inciting an insurrection by the labor unions working at Stalinallee 40, among other places?"

"Just Stalinallee 40," I said. "The rest just attached themselves on their own."

"Regardless," Mundt said "It wasn't difficult. I have an associate who tailed you once to that bar of yours. What was it called? The Aerie — yes, that's it. Ironic name, my associate said. Anyway, it didn't take him five minutes to figure out what was happening and what you were up to. He could see it all from the bar, and dope out the rest just by eavesdropping on conversations when the men came to refill their pitchers. Apparently, you made quite an impression on some of the fellas. A regular Pied Piper, I'd say."

"Laying it on pretty thick, you are."

"Just reporting what I was told," he said.

He was playing me, I understood. He was an asshole — an asshole with all of the leverage in our relationship, if you could call it that — and he was pressing. He was pressing hard, and it was working, I had to admit. I forced myself to continue my reconnoitering. I thought about the chair I was sitting on. Maybe I could stand up and grab it and fling it across the desk at Mundt. That might work.

"Don't you feel guilty?" he said. "Your friend Gerd is dead because of you."

"He's dead because of an oppressive regime that fucks the workers at every turn. He's dead because of a Soviet soldier with a rifle."

"Because of you."

"Because of your chickenshit party bosses, just a bunch of weak old men with rusty medals on their lapels, and because of their Russian overlords," I said.

"You pushed him."

"He was a grown man who made his own decisions," I said.

I looked around the room some more. There were no pictures on the wall, no other pieces of furniture. A small wire waste basket sat to the side of the desk, though. Another potential projectile, I figured. But it was out of my reach. The chair I was sitting on still made the most sense.

"You painted your friend Gerd a picture," Mundt said. "You drew him a map. Would he have acted without it? Would they all have been so riled up? Tell yourself whatever you want, but that girlfriend of yours will be burying her brother in a few days

– and that's if she's stupid enough to hang around – and you might as well have pulled the trigger yourself."

"Fuck you."

"Said the man who is seeking a favor from me."

"We have a deal, right?" I said. "Me for her, right?"

"I'm a man of my word."

"Said the double agent."

"Fair enough," Mundt said, and then he chuckled. "Fair enough."

"So, what happens now?" I said.

"You say goodbye to your girlfriend and then she walks out of here," Mundt said. "Where she goes is completely her choice. I would strongly advise her to get on the first S-Bahn after they reopen the trains going to the West. She's better off not here anymore. As I said, my offer of protection can only last for so long, after all. Better all round if she leaves. Better for me, better for her. Certainly better for her."

I looked around the room one final time — perimeter, desk, gun. I always seemed to end up looking at the pistol. Still in his lap. Still being fondled. Finger still not on the trigger. Still flaccid, then. As it were.

And then Mundt pushed back and the chair rolled away from the desk a few feet. He grabbed the pistol, then turned away from me and toward the open door that led who-knew-where. I still couldn't do anything but guess. Maybe it led to a hallway. More probably, it led to an adjacent office.

And then Mundt said, "Come on in, Elena. You heard everything, I'm sure."

34

E lena entered through the door in the back of the office. The way she looked at me, I could tell that Mundt was right. She had heard everything.

"I'll just leave you two alone," Mundt said. He pointed to the desk chair, where Elena sat, and then he left the same way that Elena had entered. Only, he closed the door. We really were alone.

My first thought was to make a run for it, but I suppressed it almost as soon as it entered my head. There was no way Mundt didn't have somebody stationed outside the office, somebody with a gun or a rifle. I would be dead before I let go of the doorknob.

Which brought me back to Elena, seated across the desk from me, seated in the position of power, armed with the knowledge of who I really was, shooting a look at me that felt at least as lethal as the gun or the rifle on the other side of the office door.

I didn't know what to say, where to begin. In the 10 seconds I considered my options, nothing sounded sincere. But as she sat there and glared, I felt I had to start.

"I was on your side, always," I said.

"Bullshit."

"I believed what you believe."

"Keep fucking telling yourself that — whatever it takes you to get through the day," Elena said.

With that, I spent the next five minutes trying to convince her that she and Gerd did what they were going to do all along — that I only steered them.

"I didn't push — I steered — and you damn well know it," I said. "And the reason I know it — and you know it, deep down — is that no man has ever forced you or talked you into doing anything that you didn't want to do in the first place. You would have bitten the head off of anybody who suggested such a thing. But now, in the biggest moment, you're saying that I somehow manipulated you? Come on. Show a little self-respect. I didn't lift you onto that table in The Aerie. I didn't make you stomp and chant."

"You fucking asshole," she said. "How dare you? My brother is dead—"

"And he was a great man, a great leader, and he died in pursuit of a great cause. His pursuit. His cause."

"Fucking asshole," Elena muttered, and then she went quiet.

I thought again about the office door, and who might be on the other side, and what he might be armed with. Maybe that was the play, despite everything. Maybe I'd catch the guard lighting a smoke or having a piss. Maybe the rifle would jam. If it was a long shot, well, I was staring directly at a no-shot if I just sat there.

Maybe, I thought. Maybe if I grabbed the wire waste basket, and opened the door quickly, and heaved it at whoever was on the other side. Maybe, as he ducked away, it would give me enough time either to tackle him or to run from him. Maybe I could scoop up the weapon. Or maybe there were two of them, in which case I would be screwed.

"Are you even German?" Elena said.

"Born in Czechoslovakia, grew up in Vienna," I said.

She said nothing.

Then I said what I meant to say all along.

"That part was always real," I said.

"What part?"

"The us part," I said.

"And what exactly was the us part?"

"It was nice. It had promise."

Elena waved her hand. She waved a second time, and wiped her eyes quickly, and said, "More bullshit."

"Not bullshit."

"Give me—"

"Not bullshit," I said.

"No? Then how did it have fucking promise, as you suggest? It was a relationship premised on an enormous lie. And what? You're telling me that you were thinking of staying once you had used us? That after the shooting ended and the smoke cleared, you were going to be here to help me pick up the pieces? Help me bury my brother — you know, your alleged friend?"

She stopped, wiped her nose on her sleeve.

"You lying sack of—"

"My feelings were real, are real," I said. "And maybe you're right. Maybe I was never going to stay. But, well, why did I stay? Why do you think I'm here? Why do you think I didn't run? Because Mundt said he had you, and I had to do something about that."

She wasn't crying any more. She was staring daggers again. Maybe it was a defense mechanism. Because even if a lot of the rest of it was indefensible on my part, this bit was not. I knew it, and she had to see it.

"I'm fucking trading my life for yours," I said. "I know you heard what Mundt said. Me for you. That's why I didn't run this morning. That's the only reason."

More daggers. Definitely a defense mechanism. That would have to be my thank-you.

And with that, the door in the back of the office opened up and Mundt walked through.

"I'm sure it was a touching reunion," he said. "And, no, I didn't listen. But now it's time, Elena. Out the other door there, and my associate will point you toward the S-Bahn. Oranienburg station. Straight down the road. It's a nice walk on a June evening."

35

Mundt sat down and then the oddest thing took place. At his instigation, we have a spy-to-spy/heart-to-heart conversation. Like two old retired spooks sharing a glass as we sat by a roaring fireplace and told all of the old stories.

I was a little surprised, to be honest. And it wasn't really like two old spies reliving their greatest hits, given that he was still fondling the pistol in his lap and all. But the way I figured it — now that I knew he had an associate outside the door — talking and talking and delaying and delaying was as good a tactic for me as any.

"So, what was it like?" Mundt said.

"What was what like?"

"The demonstration. The whole thing. Being right in the middle of it all."

"Fascinating but also terrifying," I said. I decided on honesty. I mean, as long as I didn't compromise anybody else, what the hell? Besides, the more real that I could be, the better chance I would have of sucking him in and keeping him talking.

"Why terrifying? I mean, other than the obvious."

"The tanks and the guns and the smoke?"

"Like I said, other than the obvious."

"I don't know," I said. "What scared me the most — and Gerd, too — was how nobody seemed to be in charge. I mean, somebody obviously was, but we had no idea who and no idea how the shots were being called."

"For what it's worth, my bosses think it was the Americans," Mundt said. "Then again, they don't really know. They're still looking for new britches to replace the ones they pissed in for the last day."

"You know this how?" I said.

"I was there. That was my station for the day — Karlshorst. Do you know it?"

I shook my head.

"It's in Lichtenberg," he said. "You've probably been close to it and not even known. It was an officers' mess at a Wehrmacht training school before the war, and then it ended up being the headquarters of the Soviet military bosses. It was also where the Germans officially surrendered to the Soviets. So, a lot of stuff — but yesterday might have been the all-time disgrace of the place."

"Worse than a surrender?" I said. "Hard to believe."

"Worse. I'm telling you. It was where the Politburo hid and pissed their pants while you and your union friends shook the place to its foundation."

That seemed to be a bit of an overstatement, and I told Mundt as much. Uncomfortable? Sure. Unpleasant? Absolutely. But foundation-shaking? Hardly.

"It was, like, 20,000 people confined to a city block or two," I said. "And as it turned out, they had it controlled, all done and dusted, in about an hour after the tanks showed up."

"But that's the whole point," Mundt said.

"What's the whole point?"

"The tanks," he said. "It's hard to explain what was happening. And the Politburo — Ulbricht and Grotewohl and the rest of them — they would never admit it, never say the words out loud — but you could see it in their faces."

"See what?" I said.

"The humiliation. It was devastating to watch. You see, they were all in Karlshorst, all hiding. Half of them were shitting themselves, worried that the mob would find them. I actually heard one of them say it when I was in there."

"In where?"

"I was the message-runner," Mundt said. "They got updates from the House of Ministries every 15 minutes by radio, and they would be transcribed, and I'd walk them across the big entrance hallway to the room where they were barricaded inside. Four guards at the door, two with pistols and two with rifles. I'd bring the message, one of the guards would knock, and I would wait to see that the message was handed to whoever opened the door from the other side. It would be open for 10 seconds, maybe, but it was enough to see their faces."

"And the piss dripping down their legs," I said.

Mundt nodded.

"I never knew what the messages said, but I could tell they provided no consolation. When the door opened, the mental snapshot I left with was the same: pacing, blank expressions, pale faces. And then there was the time when the door opened as I arrived with another message, and a Soviet general came out. That must have been when they told Ulbricht and the rest that the tanks were rolling."

He stopped, yawned.

"Can you imagine the humiliation they must have been feeling?" Mundt said. "They couldn't even take care of their own business by themselves. Like you said — it was big and bad but it should have been containable. Now, one thing you didn't know

— there were smaller demonstrations in other cities, too. It wasn't just Berlin. They were very aware of this, and worried it might spiral out of control. More importantly, the Soviets were very aware, too. So when the old men in the Politburo froze, well, they needed Daddy Khrushchev to get things cleaned up for them."

"Cuckolds," I said.

"Eunuchs," he said.

With that, Mundt stopped talking. I sensed that my delay tactics had ceased and that I was running out of time. I looked around the room again, saw the wire waste basket, felt the arms of the chair I was sitting on. The basket was too much of a reach. It would have to be the chair followed by a prayer.

Then Mundt suddenly stood up. He was holding the pistol as if he meant business — barrel pointed at me, finger on the trigger, no longer flaccid. He opened a desk drawer and produced a pair of handcuffs. He tossed them onto the desktop in front of me.

"Put 'em on," he said.

36

With my wrists shackled in front of me, Mundt sat down again. His finger remained on the trigger as he began talking.

"You've probably figured by now, I was really a double agent — or maybe it's a triple agent. I was pretending to work for the West but I was really working for the Stasi the whole time. I am loyal to my oath."

"Double agent, I think," I said.

"So what's a triple agent?"

"Stasi guy who feeds the West is an agent. But if he's really infiltrating the West to supply the Stasi, he's a double agent. But if the same guy goes back to the West to tell them how the Stasi is reacting to the information he's been supplying, that's a triple agent."

"Do people like that exist?"

"Beats the fuck out of me," I said. "But if we paid you enough money, I bet we might have been able to find out."

"Fuck you," Mundt said. "I was loyal to my oath."

"Yeah, yeah, and I'm sure you turned in all the cash that Gehlen paid you," I said.

He didn't answer. And exactly why I was trying to rile him up, I wasn't sure. I was just delaying, hoping for I-didn't-know-what.

"And what was the information you fed us?" I said.

"Just advance notice of things that would become public anyway, or would be readily available in time," he said. "No real harm."

"And what did your masters get in return from me?"

"Nothing from your predecessor, nothing from you," he said. "My job was just to keep tabs on you, as it were. Not really investigate or anything like that. Just be aware. And if the time came, you might provide some leverage."

"And now's the time?" I said.

"Not exactly," Mundt said. "Now's a different time. Because now, after today, I know that you have been involved in stoking the flames, as it were. I saw you myself the other day, outside the prison in Brandenburg. That's when I knew for sure. I mean, I had the intelligence from the guy in that smoky bar, but Brandenburg clinched it. There was no question after that."

I didn't know what to say. Fritz had been right, of course — right about how stupid it had been for me to go to that prison.

"Oh, Alex, you disappoint me," Mundt said. "I thought we had a true relationship — not friends, not exactly, but a relationship based upon mutual respect. And yet, you refuse to acknowledge the obvious when confronted with the evidence."

Again, I said nothing.

"Well, whatever," Mundt said. "But here is my problem. I never got around to reporting what I knew about you, and about those union men you were stoking. And, well, as you saw, things got a little out of hand today. There is much broken crockery in the streets of East Berlin that needs to be swept up, and I cannot have you be one of the shards that gets picked out of the gutter. It could end up cutting me."

"How?" I said. I knew the answer but I was still playing for time.

"It would not go well for me to be seen as having missed the fact that my contact with the West played such a role in this fiasco," Mundt said. "It's just not a good idea for my career. I'll just leave it at that — potentially not good for my future advancement. Better that you disappear."

I didn't stare at Mundt's face as he said that last bit, but at the pistol. It was in his lap, not pointed at me, but his finger was on the trigger.

I couldn't come up with a logical next question after the man had just told me that he was going to kill me. But then I thought of one.

"Disappear after a trial?" I said.

Mundt scoffed.

"Even you aren't that naive," he said. "You came to save the girl, and I can respect that — and I will keep my end of the bargain. But you honestly couldn't believe you were going to survive this."

"Actually, I did," I said. "And, actually, I could help you. I could supply you with some information about your American friends, and their role in all of this. Might help you with that career advancement you're so concerned about."

I was just throwing stuff out there. If I thought it would save me, I would give Mundt information about the RIAS guy and their role — no sweat. The value, though, would be minimal. It might not buy me give extra minutes.

One last look around the room. The wire waste basket, always a long-shot, was useless to me now, too cumbersome for a man with his wrists shackled together. Picking up the chair also seemed to be out. It might have worked if I'd had my hands resting on each arm of the chair because the first move in the lifting-and-hurling operation would not have been obvious from the start. With the handcuffs, though, my hands were in my lap. There was no way to avoid the moving hands as a prelude to the lift-and-hurl. Mundt would have shot me before I grabbed the arm of the chair.

Which left only one possibility: standing and launching myself like a missile at Mundt with my hands in front of me. If I caught him by surprise, even a little, my hands might nail him in the face and stun him just enough, and I would be on top of him, and I would do my best to beat him senseless and pray that I didn't end up gut-shot as we ended up in a pile.

As Mundt considered my proposition, I decided that it was then or never, launch and pray. It would have to be one-two-three-go. I got to about two-and-a-half, and my calves were tensed and ready to spring, and I felt the chair move, just an inch, beneath my ass.

Two-and-a-half. That was when the shot rang out from behind me, and Mundt fell backward in his chair, and a guy whose face I couldn't initially see dived over the table and kicked away the pistol and subdued him. Only when he stood up and faced me could I see that it was Max.

37

"About fucking time," I said, once I had regained my breath.

"Glad the asshole part of your personality survived the near-death experience," Max said.

He had shot Mundt in the shoulder, and that part of his shirt and jacket were being redecorated with a bright red bloom.

"Help me get him up on the chair," Max said.

I held up my cuffed wrists.

"Key?" Max said.

"The cuffs were in the top left drawer," I said.

He opened the drawer and fished out the key. I was unlocked in a second, and we lifted Mundt into a seated position. Max cuffed one hand to the chair.

Mundt looked down at the shoulder.

"I'm going to fucking bleed to death," he said.

"Yeah, you might want to apply some pressure to the wound with your free hand," Max said. "I think that's what they taught me in first-aid class."

Mundt was surprisingly with-it for someone who had just taken a bullet. His face was pretty pale, but the rest of him seemed relatively okay. His eyes were darting back and forth between Max and me. I imagined he was doing the same kind of reconnoitering that I had been doing, only from the other side of the desk. Which reminded me.

"The guy outside?"

Max replied by slashing his throat with an extended index finger.

"And did you see the woman?"

"Walking in the direction of Oranienburg, alone," Max said.

Just then, Mundt grunted loudly.

"Not having a shit there, are you?" Max said.

"Fuck you."

"Still pretty feisty. Glad to see it."

"Fuck you," Mundt said again.

"Keep it up," Max said. "And keep up the pressure, too. You're doing great — you know, for a fucking piece of shit."

Max walked around the desk to the door and poked out his head.

"Nothing?" I said.

"Just Mundt's butt buddy."

"That one?" I said, slashing my own throat.

"The one and only," Max said.

"We probably shouldn't stay long," I said.

"Relax."

"No, really."

"Let's give it a minute," Max said.

He asked about Elena, and I explained. He said, "And that's why you came here," and I nodded.

"I have to believe you've had smarter moments," he said.

I shrugged.

"Smarter but, I have to admit, probably not more honorable," he said.

I shrugged again.

"A compliment?" I said.

"Don't get used to it."

"I won't."

"I mean, it was still stupid," Max said. "And another thing. I've been tailing you since last night and you never made me. Either you were never worth a shit to start with or you're really fucking slipping. How old are you, anyway?"

"Still young enough to kick your ass."

"You'd have to catch my ass first, and that's never going to happen."

"I don't know — I'm feeling pretty spry right now," I said.

"Spry is a word that old people use," Max said.

He laughed. Mundt pushed down on the shoulder wound and grunted again, even louder this time.

"I really think—" I said.

"Just relax, old man," Max said. "I'm driving the bus right now. I know you're used to working alone, and not being the passenger, but that's the way it is in the here-and-now, in this room. So, just relax. You'll understand in a few minutes."

"Understand what?" Mundt said.

"A few minutes," Max said. "Then you'll understand, too."

38

Five minutes.

    Ten minutes.

    Mundt was losing steam, it seemed to me. The bleeding didn't seem to be a lot worse, but it must have been taking the majority of his strength to keep up the pressure. He didn't look like he was about to pass out but he did look worse.

"I really think you should drive the fucking bus out of here," I said.

"Just —" Max said, and then he was interrupted by a shadow in the doorway.

The three of us turned.

It was Fritz.

He looked at Max and said, "Everything under control?"

Max nodded.

He looked at me and said, "All in one piece?"

I nodded.

Then he walked up to the desk, put his two palms down on the surface, and leaned forward. He was about a foot away from Mundt, just staring at him. Staring and then, briefly, smiling. Mundt didn't react.

Fritz backed away and stood up straight.

"You don't know who I am, do you?"

"No fucking idea," Mundt said.

"Then let me introduce myself," he said. "My name is Fritz Ritter, and I am a proud member of the Gehlen Organization. These men work for me. In a previous life, under a previous regime, I was General Fritz Ritter of the Abwehr."

At which point, whatever color that had remained in Mundt's face drained away.

39

"I think I was in Smolensk when she died, but I've never quite been able to piece it together," Fritz said. "I mean, it was all so chaotic there at the end."

Fritz was looking at Mundt. He had taken the seat in the chair across from the desk and was talking directly to him. Mundt's face was a combination of panic and, I don't know, exhaustion. If there is such a thing. He was barely hanging on, and whatever energy he still possessed, it was being expended on that panic that became evident when Fritz introduced himself.

"Yeah, I think Smolensk when she died," Fritz said.

He paused and then acted as if a thought had just occurred to him.

"When she died," he said. "Winnie. My wife."

Peek at Max. Nothing.

Peek at Mundt. Eyes just a bit wider.

"I never knew," Fritz said. "She was healthy when I left — no diagnosis, no anything. Just Winnie."

He stopped.

"My Winnie," he said.

I wanted to say something but I had no idea what that might be. I had no idea where Fritz was going with this, and another quick peek at Max indicated he had no idea, either. Besides, it was as if Max and I weren't even in the room. We were behind Fritz, maybe 10 feet behind at that point — it was a big office. No, this was just Fritz and Mundt, face to face across the desk. It was as if they were alone. For me to say something at that point, to ask a question or whatever, would have been out of place. It would have been an intrusion, like a car backfiring outside a church.

"I didn't even find out until I finally got home to Bamberg," Fritz said. He was talking to Mundt.

"That's where we lived, Bamberg," he said. "But you already knew that, didn't you?"

With that, Mundt's eyes closed again.

"Max," Fritz said.

With that, Max backhanded Mundt — once, twice. His eyes opened again after the second belting.

"Alex," Fritz said.

"Yes, Fritz," I said.

"Come here, please."

Fritz unbuttoned his coat and reached into his shirt pocket. He took out a folded piece of paper which he handled as if it were beyond fragile. The creases on the paper were deep. Fritz unfolded it and handed it to me. It was a letter.

"Read it," Fritz said.

I started.

"No — read it out loud," Fritz said.

And so, I did.

My dearest Fritz,

I write this in what the doctor assures me will be my final week. He said the cancer was unusually aggressive. You are somewhere in Russia, I think, but the front seems to move so quickly now, based on the radio. It sounds as if it isn't far from our border. I pray for you every night and every morning. When my time comes, I imagine they will notify you in an official way, or my sister will write.

I sold the house. I know you always said you could never live here without me, and I have trusted that sentiment. The money wasn't much. It is deposited in the account. Hopefully you can get at it when this is over, whenever this is over.

One thing you should know. A Major Johannes Mundt of the SS has not been a comfort in my final days. He said you were a traitor to the Reich, and that the evidence was being assembled in some building on the Wilhelmstrasse in Berlin. He searched the house, mostly your study, and took I don't know what. He made sure that my ration cards were cut and that I was harassed. He said, "The wife of a traitor is a traitor." I was hungry but I was never more proud of you. I was never more in love.

If you have found this letter, I know you will have been back to clean out the special place. I thought about it every time I stepped on it, how it was under the third stone on the path to our little bench in the back of the garden, the one where we so enjoyed the morning sun with our coffee. As you can see, I wrapped it in an oilcloth, just as you did with your other important papers. The stone was heavy for me, weak as I am, but I eventually budged it, and this oilcloth package joined the others.

I know we will be apart at the end, but not really. Not in the ways that matter. I know I will think of us, likely in the garden. Perhaps with you wrestling an armful of the forsythia and me cutting back the top of what you were holding, and both of us laughing and saying, "But it's such a pretty yellow."

I was choked up by the time I got to the end of it. I looked at Max, and he was unashamedly wiping both cheeks. Fritz did not react much either way. He just stared at Mundt the whole time. When I finally looked from Fritz to Mundt, I saw that his head had fallen to his chest.

"Wake him the fuck up," Fritz said.

"With pleasure," Max said. He proceeded, in strict parlance, to slap the shit out of Mundt until he finally yelped. Then Max grabbed him by the hair until he yelped again.

"Now, look at the man," Max said, and then he walked back to the other side of the desk. And Mundt did look at Fritz, for maybe five seconds, before his eyes began to close again. I had never seen somebody so pale.

Fritz put his hand out, and I returned the letter. He folded it as carefully as he had unfolded it, and then he placed it back into his breast pocket — the breast pocket of his shirt, that is.

The breast pocket of Fritz's jacket held a pistol.

He stood up, and whispered, "Look at me."

Nothing.

"Look at me," Fritz said again. This time he was shouting.

When his eyes opened, Fritz fired one shot that blasted through the middle of Mundt's forehead.

Just the one shot. That was all. Just the one.

PART XV

JUNE 19

40

By the time we arrived back at the house, Fritz was too tired to stay up. Max and I downed a few and then passed out ourselves. The next morning, there was coffee and bread and butter in the living room. Max was up first, then me, then Fritz. By the time we were all together, Max began to speak.

I stopped him.

"Max, this needs to be me and Fritz, alone," I said.

"I think I'm entitled," Max said.

"You are — just not for this part," I said. "A few minutes. Please. And don't sit on the bench in the hallway, either."

Max refilled his coffee and walked down the hallway toward the kitchen. Fritz and I were left to reassemble the broken pieces, as we had done so many times before.

"You used me," I said.

"I needed you," Fritz said.

"Used me," I said.

"Trusted you," he said. "You're the only one I could trust."

"What do you mean, trust?" I said. "You didn't tell me anything."

"It was better that way," Fritz said. "And when I say trust, I guess I mean comfort or something like that. I felt comfortable knowing it was you."

He had used me before — used and then rescued. He knew it and I knew it.

"But it isn't what you think," he said. "Yes, I wanted you to be the contact with Mundt. When I found out who it was—"

"And that's why you're here in Berlin and not on the other end of a radio in Munich, right?" I said.

"Right, right," he said.

"So you dreamed up this whole operation with the unions just to get me here?"

"No, no," Fritz said. "No. You were already here. And when Mundt made the approach, and I found out who he was, his name, I just wanted you involved. So we invented a sick wife for the other agent — paperwork, hospital records, the whole shebang. But I wanted you involved."

"And you let me come this close to getting killed," I said.

"That's not fair," Fritz said. "None of us had any idea how the riot would turn out, or that the Soviet tanks would show up, or that your girlfriend would get arrested. Or that you even had a fucking girlfriend, by the way."

He stared at me. I looked down.

"The truth was, I was going to have you lure Mundt to a meeting and do it there," Fritz said. "But when all of this was happening in the last day, I had Max keep tabs on you. And when he was able to call and tell us where you were headed — he called from the station in Oranienburg — then I knew for sure. After that, we just improvised — and Max intervened as quickly as he could manage."

Fritz stopped, smiled.

"By the way — Max?" he said. "Max is good, you know? He reminds me of a younger you. Better with a weapon, a little more professional, but a little bit of a wildcard and a little bit of an asshole, too. It's a good combination."

Stop. Another smile.

"The wildcard part and the asshole part of your personality might be your best attributes, you know," he said.

Another smile.

Then a long pause.

Then Fritz said, "Do you ever think much about revenge? Like, with, you know. With Vogl?"

Werner Vogl was the Gestapo captain who killed my Uncle Otto, Fritz's great friend. Vogl also killed my pregnant wife Manon — if not actually performing the act, then creating the circumstances in which she died. I chased him right after the war, all the way to Italy, but he slipped away. It had been more than five years.

"I can't live like that," I said. "I mean, I did for a long time, but I can't anymore. Besides, he's gone, in the wind. In South America or somewhere. I just don't have the energy. The mental energy. The emotional energy."

"Yeah, I kind of agree with you there," Fritz said. "But Mundt, I don't know. I could never let it go. I never actually did anything about it but I thought about it all the time. Well, that's not totally true — I did do a few things about it. Anytime one of our agents sent back information that included a police roster or anything like a police roster, I made sure to check it out. Never saw a Mundt, though. Never once."

He got up, walked over to the table, buttered a piece of bread.

"And then he falls in my lap," Fritz said. "Just walks in off the street. The whole first day, after I saw his name in the first report, I cried. The second day, I made up a reason to come to Berlin. You had just gotten here, but I told Gehlen that you were already making great progress, and I thought it could be big, and that I wanted to monitor it on site. And that led to, well, you know. To last night."

I joined him at the table for more coffee, and I put my arm around his shoulder.

"And now, old man, how do you feel?"

"Good," Fritz said. "Not, like, elated — but I never expected elated. I'm old enough to have a sense of things, and killing somebody, well, I never expected joyful. That's just not real life."

He swallowed the last of the bread and licked an escaped bit of butter off his thumb.

"But good," Fritz said. "I don't know, peaceful. Settled, maybe. Yeah, settled."

ENJOY THIS BOOK? YOU CAN REALLY HELP ME OUT.

The truth is that, even as an author who has sold more than 300,000 books, it can be hard to get readers' attention. But if you have read this far, I have yours – and I could use a favor.

Reviews from people who liked this book go a long way toward convincing future readers of its worth. It won't take five minutes of your time, but it would mean a lot to me. Long or short, it doesn't matter.

Thanks!

I hope you enjoyed *The Berlin Uprising,* the 15th installment in the Alex Kovacs thriller series. I have also written books in two other series. One begins with *A Death in East Berlin* and features a protagonist named Peter Ritter, a young murder detective in East Berlin at the time of the building of the Berlin Wall. The other is the story of a Paris mob family in the late 1950s, beginning with *Conquest.*

Those books, as well as the rest of all three series, are available for purchase now. You can find the links to all of my books at https://www.amazon.com/author/richardwake.

And if you have any interest in joining my reading group and receiving a free novella, *Ominous Austria,* you can do that here: https://dl.bookfunnel.com/g6ifz027t7

Thanks for your interest!

Printed in Dunstable, United Kingdom